COWBOY

JULIE CAPULET

One grumpy rodeo hero. One city girl with big dreams. And enough heat to steam up the entire state of Montana.

Will Finn is the golden boy of professional bull riding. Or at least he was, until he got thrown by a rampaging bull six months ago and had to figure out how to kill some time while he got back on his feet. Now that he's made his comeback in the ring, nothing's going to slow him down.

Until Ella Parker blasts into Bozeman like a beautiful, chaotic storm. Ella's job as a New York art curator hinges on finding the next breakout artist. When she gets sent to Montana to sign rising star Fleur Jensen, Fleur drags Ella along to ... a rodeo.

Where she comes face to face with the world's hottest bull rider.

The man is sexier than sin and twice as grumpy. He's also holding the key to Ella's wildest dreams. But he's as stubborn as she is. Which means the sparks insist on making wildfire.

For Will, Ella is a distraction he doesn't need. The problem is, he's already fallen too hard to resist ...

Cowboy is a steamy standalone romance starring a hot bull rider and the sweet & sassy New Yorker who brings him to his knees. Includes two sexy fairy tale HEA epilogues! Perfect for fans of Elsie Silver and Lucy Score.

COWBOY

1

———

WILL

I WALK THROUGH THE CROWD, pulling on my worn leather gloves on as I make my way toward the cage. The bystanders move aside for me, quiet murmurs of recognition and awe filtering through my awareness, barely registering. I'm totally focused on the twenty-five hundred pounds of beast I'm about to ride as it paws the dirt and rattles the gate that'll be thrown open as soon as I'm seated on its back.

Adrenaline pumps through my veins, a surge I used to live for. Now, the high is laced with something else. Not fear. Experience. The knowledge that things can, and sometimes do, go wrong.

This will be my first ride since the accident. The fall, the broken ribs, the severe concussion, the six weeks in a hospital bed—all of it is revisiting me now in excruciating detail. *You'll bounce back,* they said. *Time to get back in the saddle, cowboy. You're too good to quit. Think of the glory.*

Eight seconds, that's all I need. No one has bested my record since I've been away and none of the amateurs here today have even made it past the four-second mark.

My name booms through the loudspeaker.

Here he is, ladies and gentleman! Will Finn is back! Six feet and three inches of grit and muscle. Just look at him! Tall. Lean. Hard. Sun-bronzed. He certainly looks up to the task at hand.

Sun-bronzed? I guess I've been called worse. Jimmy Hogan has been the announcer here at the Bozeman rodeo for as long as I can remember. The guy has a flair for the dramatic, sometimes to the point of endangering his own well-being. He's taken a beating more than once for his overly descriptive play-by-plays. Some riders get touchy about stuff like that, but it never seems to curb Hogan's style. And the audience loves it. Our rodeo attracts the biggest crowds in the state. For the bulls, for the riders, for the quality of the show, and possibly, for the unfiltered commentary.

Six months ago, ladies and gentlemen, Will Finn would have walked through his adoring crowd, tipping his hat at the girls, self-assurance radiating off him like waves. Not today, folks. No sir. Today he's stoic and contemplative, fully focused on the ride that will either make or break him. He can still feel the pain of that bone-splintering fall that's kept him out of the ring for more than half a year. No one could weather the blow of a two-ton bull stomping on their chest twice *and walk away unscathed, ladies and gentlemen. Not even the mighty Finn.*

He's messing with my concentration. Maybe I'd been too sure of myself last time. Too fucking cocky. Now, I'm wiser.

I won't make the same mistake twice.

Tuning Hogan out, I focus on the two girls walking up to me. They smile. The blond slips a folded piece of paper into my jeans pocket with two deft fingers. "Call us after your ride, Will," she says. "We'll come and ease your aches and pains."

I recognize them. Sure I do. Local girls I've partied with before. Before my fall. Before I became a recluse and discovered things about myself I never knew.

I can't quite name the feeling that thuds along with my heartbeat as I push past the girls, my eyes glued to the enormous black bull with my name on it. I feel like taking the piece of paper with their phone number on it and throwing it on the ground, grinding it into the dirt with the heel of my boot. I'm not sure what's changed in me but something has. For the first time in my life, the invitation for meaningless sex appeals to me about as much as a face-plant in the middle of the rodeo ring.

I don't like it one bit but there it is.

And Hogan's at it again. *Can Will Finn rebound to his former glory? Or will he eat dirt and end his career in a double-whammy of skull-cracking agony? Let's find out, ladies and gentlemen! Let's see if the middle Finn brother has what it takes to ride Montana's biggest, baddest rodeo steer, The King of Spades.*

Maybe the guy does have a flair for the dramatic but it's annoying as fuck to hear my own internal challenge trumpeting out through the airwaves purely for the crowd's banal entertainment.

Then again, that's what I'm here to do: to ride, to be seen, to wow, to entertain. That's my job. I might as well stop churning like a goddamn pussy and cowboy up.

It's time.

Three of my brothers are here, waiting for me, sitting at the top of the cage to help me get a secure seat. Luke is four years older, the oldest of my four brothers and my manager. "You got this, Will." He takes off my hat off and puts it on his own head. Luke's hair is dark blond, like my father's was. Mine's jet-black and wavy, like my mother's was, now stuck to my head with sweat where the hat circled.

Nathan hands me a bottle of water. I take a quick drink before handing it back. "Don't take any notice of Hogan's bullshit, Will," Nathan says. "This old brute's past his prime. Eight seconds'll be a cakewalk."

"Just relax into it," Jack adds. His straw-colored hair gleams in the sun. "Roll with him. Get the rhythm, just like you've been doing since you were five years old. You got this." I can tell they're worried for me, the accident still fresh in their minds. It was the kind of fall that could—and almost did—unhinge a career. The kind that could get under a rider's skin if he lets it. But I've been riding horses since before I could walk and riding bulls since before I could talk. I can read an animal through a kind of telepathy honed and trained almost daily over my twenty-six years. Yeah, I fucked up once but I can feel it in my bones: this ride is mine. The King of Spades is a massive hunk of power, but that's to my advantage. The bull is huge —not nimble and overly-quick, like the bull that unseated me. This is a ride I can own.

I ease myself onto the animal and lace my leather glove under the rope that's wound tight around the beast's shoulders and chest.

"Eight seconds, Will," Luke says, the words echoing through my concentration.

Eight seconds.

"You ready, Will?"

"Ready."

The signal's given and the gate swings open. The King of Spades lunges out of the cage and into the ring, bucking, springing, twisting. I relax into it, finding my rhythm. After the second lunge, and the third, predicting the bull's next move becomes easier, instinctive. A twinge in my rib reminds me of the impact and the pain of going down. My left fist clenches tighter around the rope, my right arm up, guiding my balance.

Four seconds.

The jarring, jolting glide of the dance becomes easier. Almost beautiful. Like anything is beautiful when risk, a lifetime of practice and a certain element of courage converge. I can feel all of it, burning through my veins along with the rush of the ride.

Six seconds. He's almost there! The clock is ticking but the question remains: can he hold on? The King is showing no signs of slowing down. But Finn seems almost back to his old form! He wants glory! He can practically taste it! Can he best Montana's finest?

I can hear the roar of the crowd. Hell, I can *feel* the roar of the crowd. The hum brings it all back to me. The reason I kept on riding. The thrill of victory.

And there it is. The bell. The cheers and pounding boom of the crowd on its feet.

Eight seconds! He's done it! Ladies and gentlemen, Will Finn is back!

2

ELLA

25.

The number itself might seem harmless enough in any other context except the one where it meant that I'd now spent a quarter of an entire *century* inhabiting this strange, wildly imperfect cocktail I occasionally like to refer to as my soul. This is how I pitch it to myself: twenty-five years' worth of life experience, customized knowledge and over-priced education are congregated usefully in my psyche. I'm now officially old enough to be entirely independent—not that I haven't been for far too long—and young enough to still be in the prime of my youth. Or at least this is what I try to convince myself as walk the three blocks to work on a hot August morning in New York City.

I'm in a surly mood this morning. First, the quarter century thing. Also, my dreams were especially vivid last night, starring...*cowboys*, of all things, which I blame on a series of erotic romance novels I've developed a secret addiction for. Those rugged, fictional heroes with their big cocks and bad attitudes are just so wildly entertaining. I woke tangled in my sheets, soaked in sweat. It's embarrassing to even think about.

Before I can entirely convince myself that a quarter-century's worth of valuable and hard-won experience is about to infuse gigantic amounts of good fortune, mostly-wholesome fun and at least one intelligent bo-hunk with killer abs and a great sense of humor into my life, I arrive at work where my boss, James, is waiting for me. I work at an upmarket art gallery. My boss is the owner of the gallery and is—how should I put this—a total prick.

"What do you want first, Ella?" James says. "The good news or the bad?"

"Good morning, James. Uh, let's see. The good, I guess?"

James launches straight into it. "I'm sending you to the Fleur Jensen exhibition. In Bozeman." This causes me to do a double-take. Did I hear that correctly? "Wherever Bozeman is. I've got to get ready for the Ransom show and I need Astrid here to help me. Her eye is impeccable." *And I have an all-access pass to her bed too, which means she stays put.* Jerk.

I know what he's referring to, of course. River Ransom is the hottest new artist of the season. I somehow managed to secure him for a solo exhibition. Astrid and I are both assistant curators, both twenty-five. The difference between Astrid's lowly status and mine is that Astrid happens to be getting down and dirty with the boss—a detail I do *not* envy her for, even if she does get to help set up the Ransom show, which will no doubt be spectacular.

"Bozeman?" A ripple of something I can't identify swirls through my gut. "Isn't that in Montana?"

"Somewhere like that. Or Idaho. I can never keep those two straight. Normally I'd go myself but I'm obviously too busy right now. You'll need to leave on Friday morning. The blond travel agent on the corner organized your ticket. I had her email it to you. If you want to finish early to go home and pack, that would be fine. Astrid and I can finish up here."

Pack?

James is still talking. "What I want you to do is sign Fleur Jensen for the November exhibition. She's had some big sales lately and her trajectory is impressive. Do you think you're up to it?"

James is a condescending asshole, but the slant of the sunlight suddenly feels like it's been infused with something hopeful.

I'm not entirely sure why.

There are cowboys in Montana.

Aren't there?

Of course it's idiotic to get even mildly excited about this. Now that I think about it, I read an article about

Bozeman once that mentioned it was one of the wealthiest towns in the west. It's probably full of turtleneck-wearing yuppies who drive Range Rovers that never get muddy. Maybe cowboys have all been phased out by now. Maybe they only exist in Brad Pitt movies and steamy romance novels.

"Probably." Then I remember my boss hasn't finished doling out life-changing pronouncements, and I have a feeling I know what's coming. "What's the bad news?"

"I'm sure you realize your contract expires at the end of the month…" He looks almost genuinely remorseful for a milli-second but then it's gone. "Sorry, Ella, but we won't be renewing it." *We.* Him and Astrid, I can only assume. "Our turnover is still down and I can't afford to keep both of you on."

I glance at Astrid. She has shiny blond hair she wears short, like a seventies bowl cut. Styled, it looks hip and modern, but now, tousled from a recent romp with James, possibly, it looks weird. Her round, hazel eyes are apologetic. We're friends and I like her. We've worked together for two years and we're close, as these things go. Occasionally we go for drinks after work on the Friday nights when James is busy.

It's not her fault I'm getting fired.

James is still talking, to the wall, where he adjusts a hook. "If you sign Fleur, I *might* be able to keep you on through November. But after that, I can't make any promises."

This is exceptionally bad news. I have massive student loans to repay and can barely afford the mortgage, taxes and maintenance on the two-bedroom apartment I inherited in SoHo, which I share with my roommate Sadie. Since I've worked at Heights Gallery for almost two years, I might get a small redundancy pay-out, but it'll cover one or two months of my bills, if that. And even though the market is insane right now, I'd rather be dragged out by repo men than even consider selling my apartment. I was born in that apartment. It belonged to my grandparents and then my parents, all of them now gone. There are far too many memories oozing out of those exposed brick walls to even consider selling. I'd sell my soul before I sell my apartment.

Sadie works for an independent film company and also has massive students loans to pay. We eat ramen noodles for dinner at least three times a week and buy our work clothes off strategically-scouted sale racks.

I really can't afford to lose my job, is what it boils down to.

Maybe the ranches in Montana are hiring.

Sure. And maybe a phantom cowboy will sweep me off my feet and take me for a ride on his black stallion. He'll have big, sweaty muscles and an enormous—

"Ella?"

"Oh. Sorry, what?"

"The travel agent down at the corner is expecting you," James says, interrupting my mini-joy ride. "Your flights, hotel and rental car have already been booked. It won't be overly deluxe, unfortunately. A Super 8 or some such. The ticket is for carry-on only and if you exceed the weight limit you'll have to pay for the extra baggage yourself. Rent-a-Wreck was very reasonable. You'll be picking your car up at the airport. I wouldn't have bothered with it if it wasn't completely necessary but apparently Montana is..." James pauses, taking a step back to assess the alignment of the hook he's hanging.

"Big?" I venture.

"Yes." Dismissively. Then something occurs to him and he glances briefly in my direction. "You can drive, right?"

"Um...yes, I have a license." I've only driven a couple of times. There's no need to tell him about that small fender bender I got into (actually it wasn't that small but no one was hurt, which is the main thing).

"And if you can't get Fleur to sign, well, I'm afraid I won't be able to pay you past the end of the month."

"I'll get her to sign." It's the first day of August. If I can secure Fleur for November, that'll give me four more months of employment. Plenty of time to find something else to pay my bills.

"I've left your ticket open-ended for now," James continues. "You can book the return flight as soon as you get Fleur to sign, which could take a few days. Apparently she's already refused two New York offers. She's holding out for the big time, since she knows she's got the street appeal."

"I'll pin her down," I tell him. James and I both know it was me who not only found the artists for five of the past six shows, but also clinched the deals. The process of signing an artist can be a painstaking one. Wooing a moody, temperamental ego that's being flirted with by pushy curators all over town can take weeks and involve pep talks, bribery and all manner of creative coercion. I don't know if I possess a talent or just an über-determined enthusiasm, but for some reason I usually come out on top. I can be convincing when I put my mind to it.

"You're going to make her an offer she can't refuse," James says. "And if she *does* refuse, you're going to be persistent. You're not going to take no for an answer."

"Right."

Maybe a little jaunt to the outer reaches of the Wild West is exactly what I need, cowboys or no cowboys. Maybe Big Sky country will kick-start my life into new and fabulous directions.

The gallery phone rings and James answers it, then disappears into the back office to talk. Astrid's looking at me with a soulful expression I can't quite read. She shoots a quick look toward the office door, which is now closed. "Ella," she begins earnestly, like she's been planning what she's about to say for a while. "We both know the only reason I get to keep my job is because I'm sleeping with the boss."

I silently agree with her but don't say so. I want to hear where Astrid's going with this.

"You're really good at this job, Ella," she says. "*Really* good. You've got a killer eye for this shit, and I mean that. Every artist *you* find sells for much higher prices than either my picks or James's—and *every single one* of the exhibitions you've curated has completely sold out, with crazy-ass profits. River Ransom was your discovery, we all know that. You found his painting on that obscure website last year, remember? And I really don't think he would've agreed to come to us if you hadn't been the one to talk him into it."

I've had these thoughts myself, of course. I even played around with the idea of asking for a raise at one point. Now that I've basically been fired I guess there isn't much chance of that happening.

"Ella, you should borrow the money and start your own gallery. If you do, I'll jump ship. If you'd want me, that is. I'd do it myself but I don't have the same kind of talent you have. All it would take was one stellar opening show and you could make back all the money it would take to start the business. Look at River—his paintings are selling for twenty thousand dollars each. How much would it take to start a gallery? A hundred thousand? One fifty? *Think* about it, Ella. Twenty paintings at thirty percent commission and you're looking at *a hundred and twenty thousand dollars*. For *one* show."

I'm a little shocked by Astrid's gush. She's obviously given this a lot of thought.

"And you found Fleur Jensen, too," she continues. "*You* were the one who first saw her on that online gallery. Do you remember what you said about her? You said, 'We should get her now before she gets too big.' Do you know how rare that is? Do you know how lucky you are, to do what you can do? To just take a line-up of paintings and say: *that* one. *That's* the artist that's going to sell for megabucks, out of all these other millions of paintings and painters who are trying to get noticed. *I* can't do that. James can't even do that! We're just *guessing*. But you *know*. You have a knack for it. You should totally capitalize on that knack."

Wow, Astrid is worked up. She's been plotting. Things between her and James must be worse than I thought. She wants out of her relationship but breaking it off would also mean losing her job. I know how badly Astrid needs her paycheck, just like I need mine.

"At least think about it, okay? Go to Montana, Ella, and secure Fleur Jensen, if you can. But not for James. Get her for yourself. Or get someone else. Someone even better."

Shit. Astrid is desperate. Until now, I'd never seen evidence of a vengeful bone in Astrid's lithe, pale-skinned little body. But she's serious. She's practically pleading. As if *I* might be her salvation.

It's a strange turn of events. Here I am, suddenly on the cusp of an impromptu journey that might turn out to be life-changing, in more ways than one.

"You really think I could do it?" I hear myself asking.

"Ella, I *know* you can do it." We're locked in this strange, intense little connection, with me sort of drinking in her encouragement and Astrid communicating a sparked urgency that practically shoots in flamboyant rays out of her eyes. I get the strange sense that Astrid is somehow relying on me. Which is weird.

Except that I realize she's right.

Because the thing is: I know I can do it too.

"Of course I'd want you on board." I give her a heartfelt hug.

"Keep me posted, okay?"

"Sure. I'll see what I can do. If I can sign her, we'll work through all the details as soon as I get back."

It's a long shot, of course. About a million variables have to align in perfect symbiosis for my pipe dream to even get close to becoming a reality. But, hell, I might as well take the first step. Which, after the dizzyingly outrageous events of the past five minutes, happen to be boarding my jet to Yellowstone.

"He's had a lawyer look at your contract, Ella. He found a loophole which means he can get out of paying you the small redundancy. If he fires you at the end of the month, that's it. He didn't even want to give you the two weeks' notice. And even if you do convince Fleur, he might fire you as soon as the deal is signed. Go get Fleur, Ella. But not for him. Get her for yourself."

"That—"

"Here he comes."

That *bastard*.

So I say my goodbyes, receive another mini-lecture about the art of the deal from my slithery employer, then, still dazed, I walk out of the gallery and take a left, go home to pack my carry-on, making sure to include my snazziest pair of high-heeled cowboy-type boots, no doubt perfect for the frontier.

Wow. I'm going to Montana. I've never been west of Cincinnati.

I've never packed up only what I can fit in my carry-on and gone on a wild, out-West adventure.

To a place where there might—just might—be the opportunity to see a real live cowboy in his natural habitat.

If such a thing even exists.

I guess I'm about to find out.

Look out, Bozeman. Here I come.

3

———

WILL

THE PARTY'S in full swing, to celebrate my return to glory.

The only problem is, the last thing I feel like doing is partying.

I've changed during my forced hiatus from the rodeo circuit. The six weeks in the hospital didn't change me. I barely even remember most of that. I was too drugged up.

It was the four and a half months between then and now that awakened some hidden corner of my psyche I never even knew existed. Maybe the knock on the head triggered some latent talent that was waiting there all along.

During those long days of recovery, when I couldn't ride my horses or work the ranch, like I've done every day of my entire life, I found myself at a loose end. Left alone in the house or in my cabin, forced by circumstance to rest. Days when this crazy obsession took hold, surprising me not only with the intensity of it but also the results.

I'm not quite ready to share my secret with the wider community I inhabit. But it's on my mind.

All the time.

I find myself wanting to get back to it. Now.

Which pisses me off.

This isn't me. I was never a player or a party animal, but I knew how to have a good time, at least. Now I seem to have morphed into a fucking recluse with the urge to hide myself away and revel in my new discovery.

"Hey, Will." It's Fleur Jensen, my brother's girlfriend. One of only two people, in fact, who knows about my secret. Nathan knows too. Nate is a year older than me. We've always been close. We've both known Fleur since we were kids. She grew up on the ranch that borders ours. Once, she was a skinny little girl with white-blond pigtails. Now, she has long platinum hair and smoky blue eyes. Fleur is beautiful but doesn't flaunt it. She's too much of a tomboy for that. To me, she feels like a sister. She's a painter who has made a name for herself in the local art scene and is beginning to get some recognition from further afield. "That was some ride."

"Thanks."

Fleur, I know, can ride a bull better than most men. Not that she's interested in competing in the ring anymore, doing barrel races or lasso tricks, like she was as a kid. Now she's focused on her art career. In fact she has an exhibition in town this week. "You coming tomorrow night?" she asks me.

She's trying it on again, pushing me to do something I've already made clear I'm not about to do. Because she is like a sister and because I've known her most of my life, she knows she can get away with things most people can't. "Nope. I'm busy."

"Doing what?" She's watching my expression, knowing full well I'm avoiding the topic.

"Jerking off, hopefully," says Nathan, appearing out of the crowd. He slings his arm around Fleur's shoulders. "This hermit gig is getting a little old, bro. You need some action to help take the edge off that horrendous mood. What's the big deal, anyway? Why do we have to keep all this stuff quiet?"

"Because I asked you to." I finish off the last of my beer. I glance at one of the many women eyeing me up. I could take my pick. I scan the open-plan living room of my family's house. It's a huge room, with a stone fireplace taking up most of the northern wall, high ceilings displaying wooden beams that were cut and hauled by my great grandfather. The hanging deer-antler chandelier was my father's pride and joy. Expansive windows look out across the five thousand acres of my family's ranch.

The house is packed full of people, loud with music and conversation as the alcohol flows and the party gets looser. Wyatt, my youngest brother, is in the corner surrounded by girls. Jack is on the couch, also being hounded. We've all got the same allure, apparently. They travel for miles and descend on us in droves, which is hardly something to complain about.

I can see that almost every woman in the room is aware of me, trying to get my attention. The rodeo hero is back on top. I'm 6'3" and built. I have black hair and green eyes. I make the most of what I've been born with. Or at least I used to.

A girl joins us. "Hi, Will. I'm Jessie. I've followed your career for ages. *God*, you were *so* awesome today. That ride was just...*so* awesome." Mildly irritating. "That bull was *gigantic*, and so mean-looking! But you made it look easy. You're *such* a good rider."

"Yeah, Will," Nathan adds, elbowing me. "You're *so* awesome."

I ignore him, wishing I was anywhere but here.

The groupie is doing absolutely nothing for me. Why does every single one of them have to be so fucking *easy*?

I should be glad. I should be thanking my goddamn lucky stars that women are willing to jump into bed with me any time I flick them a half-interested glance.

But it's all so damn predictable. I know exactly how it'll play out if I go with it. She'll give and I'll take. I'll use her then move on as soon as I've had my fill. She might entertain a glimmer of hope that I'll call her again, but deep down she'll already know I won't. She doesn't care. "You're even hotter up close," she coos, touching my shirt.

I glance down at her. Her top is low-cut and practically see-through. I feel the smallest flicker of lust—not for her in particular, but just ... someone. It's strange, though. My lust is more about the waning adrenaline high and the euphoria of my win. I have this unfamiliar urge to share it with someone I actually care about.

"Will, there's something I want to show you," Jessie says. Her fingers graze mine.

"You don't say," Fleur murmurs, looking mildly disgusted.

"And there's something *I* want to show *you*," Nathan says to Fleur, leading her away. "Later, kids."

Fleur looks back at me. "Will, if you change your mind about tomorrow night—" They disappear into the crowd.

The music is loud and Jessie's saying something.

"What?" I lean closer. She smells of cheap perfume and I can't help it, I pull back. I feel sort of sick.

What the fuck is up with me?

Usually by now I'd be dragging her upstairs. Or maybe rolling around in the hay with this chick plus a couple of her friends. Tonight it's all I can do not to storm back to my house and wallow in my own dissatisfaction. Why can't I find someone who's even remotely on my wavelength? Why does it always feel so one-sided?

I never used to worry about shit like this, but things have changed. *I've* changed. Since the accident. All of a sudden I want more. And I'm starting to wonder if I'll ever find it.

"Is it true what they say about you?" Jessie purrs.

"Depends on what you've heard."

"You're a legend. And I'm not just talking about rodeo, Will."

I guess I've earned myself some kind of reputation as a good fuck. Hardly breaking news.

The groupie is getting bolder. "Show me your room," she whispers. Her fingers touch my chest. I take a step back. For a split second, I consider taking her hand, leading her down the track behind the main house toward the river to my log cabin.

But I can't do it.

I can't fucking do it.

"I've ... uh ... I've got some other plans tonight."

She's undeterred. "Just for a minute, Will. It won't take long."

That's the problem. I don't want a quickie.

What I want is something *real.*

Her fingers touch my arm again and I have this raging urge to brush them off. Roughly. *What the fuck is wrong with me?*

"I've had the biggest crush on you, like, *forever.* I mean, everybody does, right? The way you rode that bull, oh my *god.* Tell me what you want me to do, Will." She leans closer. "I'll give you anything you want."

These girls. Don't they have any self-respect?

"Maybe another time."

Just go with it, man. Pretend she's the love of your goddamn life for an hour. Pretend this means something more.

Jessie pulls out her phone. "Are you on Snap? I'd love to message you."

Fuck. "I've got to go. Goodnight, Jessie." I walk away without so much as a backwards glance. She calls after me but I ignore this, and everything else. I wish I didn't feel so damn lonely.

I slip out the back door and into the night. I walk down the path that leads to my cabin. It's a roomy four-bedroom, two-story wrangler's cottage, built for the hired help my father once needed, before his five sons were old enough to become useful on the ranch. I moved into it just recently, after the accident. As I healed and became stronger again, I cleaned it up, moved my stuff into it, along with a few pieces of furniture. My brothers all recognized that I needed my own space, as part of my "healing process," the doctors called it. Whatever. But it's true. My need for privacy is a new development. After the fall, my brothers were so glad I was alive, they would have allowed me anything. We lost our parents in a gruesome car crash ten years ago. For a few days after I'd been gored and stomped on by that bull, the doctors weren't sure if I was going to make it. My brothers were told it was unlikely I'd ever ride again.

Somehow, I've proved them wrong.

But grit is something we all have. It's just a part of the way we were raised. Ranch life calls for it, and after the death of our parents, we got tougher. We had a ranch to run and work to get on with.

The night is clear, and warm. A billion stars are out, splashed across the sky like a smattering of glowing white paint against a black canvas.

Yellow light from a lamp I left on illuminates the windows as I approach my cabin. I like the look of it, with all its isolated, rough-hewn appeal. I open the door and run up the stairs, to the loft, which is one big room that takes up the entire second floor.

I can't wait to get started.

4

ELLA

AND THIS IS how I find myself, two days after my 25th birthday, disembarking from a small commuter plane and stepping out onto the tarmac of Big Sky country.

It's easy to see how it earned its name. Bright, cloudless skies shine over majestic green hills with a backdrop of craggy mountains. The vista is framed by an enormous panoramic blue dome of sky.

As I make my way to the Rent-a-Wreck rental car desk, my eyes rove the airport population discreetly for—yes—cowboys.

I look around, checking out everyone who hasn't just gotten off my flight (I've already checked them out). But I can't see anyone that might fit the cowboy description. Not even close. These people look like ... regular people.

Where are all the cowboy hats? The sexy leather

chaps? Those cruel, pointy things they wear strapped to their boots to make their horses run faster?

Once I get my car keys, I walk out to the parking lot to find my ride. It's even more of a piece of shit than I might have expected. Even so, it could be worse. James could have insisted on coming with me.

I put my carry-on in the back seat of the car, climb into the driver's seat and fire up Google maps. The exhibition starts at seven and it's already 6:29. True to form, James requested the cheapest flight to Bozeman which meant I changed planes twice. Even so, my enthusiasm is somehow still intact even after surviving ten hours of airport hell. Firstly, James will (hopefully) be my boss for a limited amount of time, which might possibly end in a matter of days. Second, I'm in *Montana*. And feeling every ounce of my fresh air high.

My phone pings.

Don't come back without those paintings!

Jesus.

James is barraging me with angry little text-threats.

I'll do my best! I text back. Then I delete his message, just like I deleted the four he sent earlier. *Asshole.*

Carefully, in an attempt not to re-create the fender bender that's still fresh in my mind, I navigate my way out of the airport parking lot and start heading east.

The landscape is vast. Desolate-looking but beautiful, too. When you're used to the sky-tall concrete jungle, something about Montana makes you feel free and completely unconfined. This *is* exactly what I needed, I decide. A break from life. An uninhibited adventure across the prairie, like Laura Ingalls Wilder with money issues and an art obsession. My Rent-a-Wreck isn't all that much more technologically advanced, after all, than a stage-coach. And far less comfortable, I'd wager.

Bozeman isn't far. By 6:53, I'm driving into the town.

It's cute and rustic, like something straight out of a Clint Eastwood movie. I wonder if there's a saloon, if they still have those. Squat brick and wooden buildings line the wide main street. People are walking around looking—again—like regular people, disappointingly. I might as well be in freaking upstate New York.

But then I see the sign for the Blackbird Gallery and pull up in front of it. It only takes me four tries to paral-lel-park my car. It's the size of a tin can and looks ridiculous wedged between two fuck-off pickup trucks, but whatever. With its *Rent-a Wreck!* logo emblazoned across one of its dented doors, it's practically begging for its fate.

I sling my faux leopard skin Prada bag (seventy percent off at Macy's, thank you very much) over my shoulder and walk into the gallery.

Inside, the gallery is crowded, bustling with hip-looking people. Still no cowboy hats but there are a few people wearing cowboy boots, so that's at least something.

And there's a Western vibe to the place I'm really starting to dig.

Music is playing and the noise of lively conversation fills the space.

Fleur Jensen's paintings look even more impressive in person than they did online. Their colorful landscape scenes catch your eye and hold it, just like that first painting did when I saw it on one of the many online galleries I scour daily. As Astrid pointed out, it would have saved us a lot of trouble if James had listened to me then. Then again, if he had, I wouldn't be here now.

I'm greeted by a woman with a brown bob and round glasses. "Welcome to the Fleur Jensen exhibition," she says. "I'm Amanda Riggs. I own the gallery."

"Hi, I'm Ella Parker, from New York. We spoke on the phone yesterday."

"Oh yes, I remember. You've come to try to lure Fleur to the big city." She chuckles throatily. "You might need to get in line. There are at least three other New York scouts here. As well as two from L.A. and one from Chicago."

I smile back, accepting a brochure from Amanda and a glass of champagne from a passing waiter. There's no need to discuss my plan with any of my competitors, including Amanda. I'll save the sales pitch for Fleur herself.

"You've done a fabulous job with the display." I don't bother mentioning she could easily be selling these paintings for twice the price.

"Thank you," she smiles. "Fleur is over there if you'd like to meet her. She's the one in blue."

I know who she is. I've done my research.

It'll be a while before I get anywhere near Fleur. She's surrounded, and I need a little more time to perfect my pitch. I have to make absolutely sure she understands why mine is the only offer she should seriously consider. So I take my time, browsing, studying each painting in turn.

I recognize a few other people in the room. Alistair Johnson, a New York talent scout, and Roxanne Mayberry, who's the head curator at another SoHo gallery.

Waiting for my moment, I keep an eye on Fleur.

I can't help but notice that a man is standing next to her, leaning against a wall with his burly arms folded. He's watching her with cool, attentive possessiveness, like he's not at all happy about people getting so close to her. He looks like he's considering lunging at anyone whose intentions rub him the wrong way. Every now and then Fleur gives him a little kiss on his chiseled jaw, as though to placate him. His eyes spark every time she touches him.

It's impossible not to notice that Fleur's boyfriend is, well, seriously hot. He's by far the closest thing I've seen to a cowboy so far. He has dark brown hair and is tall and built—and I mean *built*, not just work-out-during-lunch-break type built—with a deep tan, like he spends most of his time outside doing hard, dirty physical work.

Is he a ranch hand?

He's outshining the art and I wonder abstractly where his ilk might hang out. I'm sure I'll never know him and I don't specifically want to but it's a nice change. To be able to admire from afar that rare, smoldering energy of a roughed-up alpha male of our species. It feels downright hopeful, bumping into one, providing proof that they actually do exist.

Fleur is gorgeous. Her press photos don't do her justice. Another thing I plan on fixing, if she agrees to sign with me. She has long, white-blond hair that hangs to her waist and a Western glamor New York stylists would drool over. Not staged, authentic, real. No wonder the beefy boyfriend is more than a little smitten.

I basically chug another glass of champagne, then I take my chance once the crowd begins to clear out. Forcing myself to be courageous and taking my own fate by the balls, I dive right in. "Hi, Fleur. I'm Ella Parker. I'm a huge fan of your work. I'm opening a gallery in New York City that's going to be the most sought-after in town. I'd love for you to exhibit with me in October." It's the first time I've said it out loud and it feels ... good.

Fleur smiles and her boyfriend steps closer. I watch as his arm slides around her waist. "You and every other New Yorker, sweetheart." His comment is aggressive, and snide. And sexy as fuck. I decide I'm just as big a fan of the boyfriend as I am of Fleur herself.

"Easy, Nate." Fleur kisses his jaw, which is rough with

his five o'clock shadow. *Damn.* You just don't see his type in New York. Sun-tanned and muscle-bound and gloriously mussed-up. Maybe he could introduce me to a few of his friends during my short visit to the frontier. "Nice to meet you, Ella. This is Nathan. Please, tell me more."

"I guarantee I'll get you the highest possible prices for your paintings," I say.

Nathan eyes me skeptically. "What kind of prices?"

"Fifty thousand each. And for the best five out of twenty I'll run an auction starting at a hundred thousand each. Which could go sky high if we play our cards right."

Nathan whistles and Fleur's eyebrows shoot up.

"Seriously?" Fleur asks. "How? These painting are only selling for fifteen. Some are listed for ten."

"They're worth a lot more," I tell her. "You're under-selling yourself. You've got talent to burn, Fleur. If you'd let me, I could put you right in the middle of the New York spotlight. Which is the only spotlight that matters." Sure, I occasionally come across as a little arrogant when it comes to my hometown, but it's true. New York *is* the center of the art world. I live and breathe art every day. It's my job and my obsession. If there's one thing I know, it's how to spot a winner. And these are winners.

"I'll have to think about it," she says. "I've had a lot of other offers."

I like Fleur. She seems grounded, and smart. "Of course. Take your time. But none of them will even be in this ballpark, I can assure you. Alistair over there will probably offer you twenty each. Roxanne will go one better, possibly promising twenty-five. I can more than double whatever they offer you. And if you're interested in signing with me for October I'll fill you in on exactly what we'd need to do to launch you into the stratosphere. The sooner we start, the higher the prices will go."

"It sounds tempting," she admits. "But how can you be so sure?"

"You're one of the best I've ever seen, Fleur," I tell her honestly. "I've been responsible for sourcing and selling ninety percent of the profits at the gallery I've worked at for the past two years. I'm about to branch out on my own, which will give me more freedom to market you to the next level. I'd get you featured in a few of the big magazines. We'd run a series of strategic ads. We'd offer key people invites to the exhibition opening and we'd spread the word that you're the new It girl. We'll create a buzz so electric, people will get hungry. The glitterati love outdoing each other. Once the buzz gains momentum around town, prices will start to skyrocket." I'm finding my groove, I realize. I actually sound like I know what I'm talking about.

And I've already made the crucial decision. James won't agree to the terms I'm presenting to Fleur. My terms are far better. I want to work with Fleur and make her a star, something James would limit, because it's always more about him than it ever has been about his artists.

All I need to do now is to find a prime location in SoHo that's the perfect size, available, visible and affordable, get a few stellar advance offers on Fleur's paintings, apply for a colossal bank loan to pay for the deposit and interior styling upgrades and ... I'll be a fully-fledged owner of my very own art gallery.

Shit. Can I really pull this off?

"I've decided I like this girl," Nathan says to Fleur.

It's slightly pathetic how flattered I am that Nathan likes me, or at least likes my offer. It makes me want to succeed even more. Maybe it's the cowboy boots or the cocky alpha arrogance. Most men in the New York art scene are either ego-inflated dickheads like James or tepid softies, like most of the men I've ever dated. Or they're flamboyantly gay. Maybe that's also why my imagination has been running away with me lately, and leading me headlong into the smutty pages of my new favorite pastime, where a lot of hay bales have to be thrown around in the hot sun by well-hung—

"Ella?"

Oh. Fleur is saying something. "Sorry, what?"

"I said we're heading back to my place for dinner. Would you like to come? We could talk a little more about your offer."

"I'd love to."

Maybe Fleur has a brother. Or maybe Nathan does.

5

WILL

I STAND BACK to look at the painting I'm working on.

It's done.

Possibly the best one I've done yet.

I don't know a lot about this stuff but I have a feeling these are pretty good. Not that I'll ever bother finding out. I can just imagine what Jimmy Hogan would do with that kind of information. *Will Finn, our favorite rodeo hero, has a secret little hobby he never told us about. Who knew our champion was a closet Picasso? Apparently,* that's *what he's been doing behind closed doors when he was out of commission on the rodeo circuit. Painting pretty pictures.*

It's the last thing I want anyone finding out about. I'm not sure why. Maybe because it feels personal. Like I'm finally tuning into some of the emotion that went along with losing my parents. They were the kind of parents everyone wishes they had. Cool, successful, glamorous, lucky. Until that one fateful day when everything changed.

Or maybe it has something to do with almost dying when I got trampled by a two-ton bull. Or finally realizing that I'm twenty-six years old and I've never had a relationship that lasted more than a week. Or suddenly feeling like I want more out of life than sex with groupies I can't actually stand to have a conversation with.

Fuck.

Maybe I'm getting weak.

Maybe that fall fucked me up more than I realized.

It pisses me off that my secret's out. Nathan turned up a couple of months ago and ran upstairs before I could stop him. I was so immersed in the music and the paint I hadn't noticed until it was too late. He barged into my studio. At first he was stunned. Staring at the stack upon stack of paintings. Then he laughed a little, which is exactly what I would have expected him to do. *I* would've fucking laughed at *him* if the tables were turned.

We work on the ranch. We ride and train and sell horses. We herd and tend to our many thousands of head of cattle. We conquer bulls in the ring. We drink whiskey and get dusty and dirty and we swear a lot.

We don't paint goddamn pictures.

I have no idea why I feel so compelled to do exactly that.

It's actually not a new feeling. It's just one I've buried for a long time.

There's this electricity inside me that wants out. It almost hurts sometimes if I don't let it have its way. It feels a lot like *lust*, this urge. Hot, necessary, needy. Channeling itself out of the end of my paintbrushes, like a release. When I scratch the paint along the surface of that canvas, letting it build and seeing how the image plays out, it feels so fucking good to just go with it.

What ends up on the canvases when I'm done is borderline crazy. It feels raw and emotional.

Maybe because his girlfriend is an artist, Nathan thinks of himself as something of an expert. "You know, man," he drawled, after leafing through some of the two hundred or so paintings accumulating in my loft. "These are actually pretty fucking good. Let me show some to Fleur."

"No," I said. "I paint to let off steam. When I couldn't work after the fall it gave me something to do, but I'm not showing anyone. I'll probably burn them all at some point. Until then, no one hears about this. I mean it, Nate. I'm swearing you to secrecy. Or I'll fucking kick your ass."

At that exact moment, there was a knock on the door downstairs. Before I could stop him, Nathan called out to Fleur, goddamn him. "I can't keep secrets from her anyway, Will. Let her see these."

Next thing I knew, there she was, standing in my loft.

Her eyes went wide. She just walked around, staring, sort of speechless for a few minutes. Which pissed me off.

"Jesus, Will," she finally said. "These are *incredible*."

So I swore them *both* to secrecy. "This is between the three of us and no one else. I don't want all of goddamn Montana in on it. I'm trusting you two to keep it to yourselves."

Nathan knows I can take him in a fight. I'm an inch taller than him and stronger, even though he's quicker. Fleur, though, is another story. I can trust my brothers because I can threaten them. Women are a whole different ball game and one I don't pretend to understand. I'm not naïve enough to think I can control her, as politely as I might ask.

There's also the small matter of owing her some money for a horse I bought from her old man last week that I haven't gotten around to paying for yet.

"Give me three paintings," she said. "That's what I want as payment."

"No."

"Yes. Those are my terms. I promise not to tell a single soul who painted them."

"No."

"Please?" She stares up at me with pleading blue eyes.

Fuck it. "Fine," I say gruffly. "But if you breathe a word about this to anyone I'll storm over there and burn them to a smoking pile of ash."

She was still staring at one of my paintings. A charging bull. "You could sell these—"

"Would you drop it, please?" By that point I was thoroughly irritated. "Get out, both of you."

So, as it turned out, against my better judgement, Fleur took three of the paintings. As long as they keep their word, everything will be fine.

I don't know if I'll end up burning all my art. I've gotten attached to a few of these paintings. They remind me of things. Of thoughts I've had, and memories. Dreams. Hopes, even.

I'm thinking about doing a series but it would involve some outside help. I've tried to use photographs but it's not the same.

I need a model.

Of course I won't get one. The very last thing I need is another groupie wanting to strip off her clothes and jump into bed with me while I'm trying to paint a goddamn picture.

Fuck, would you listen to yourself, man? You've turned into a fucking pussy.

Goddamn it.

I toss the paintbrush I'm holding into some water and go downstairs. I grab my hat and go outside to find my horse.

I need some air and good long ride, alone under the big sky.

6

ELLA

I FOLLOW Nathan's monster truck to Fleur's house, driving with meticulous precision. It takes about forty minutes and the last ten are along a teeth-jarringly bumpy gravel road. It's getting dark and I almost go hurtling off the road twice. I manage to avoid death only because I drive at around twenty miles an hour the entire way. But we finally make it.

"Holy *hell*, where'd you learn how to drive?" asks Nathan grouchily as I'm getting out of my car.

"Oh. Yeah, sorry about that. I usually take the subway."

Nathan stares at me then just shakes his head and walks away. Fleur's a lot nicer. She invites me into her cute little cottage, which is made of wood and glass and stone. It's rustic but also modern. Any New Yorker would kill to have a space like this. I decide I like Montana. A lot.

"Nathan is going to fry up some steaks while you and I

talk." Fleur invites me to sit on one of the leather couches arranged in front of the stone fireplace. "Honey," she says to Nathan. "Could you open a bottle of wine?"

Hot, surly, rugged *and* a cook? Kill me now. I have *got* to find myself one of these.

Nathan pours three glasses of red wine and then disappears into the kitchen.

"I love your house," I tell her.

"Thanks. My parents live in the big house, on the other side of the ranch. So I get the cottage. I love it. I don't think I could ever move."

"I can see why."

I'm looking around for more of Fleur's art and she seems to read my mind. "If you're looking for more of my paintings, I used them all for the exhibition. Which is something I wanted to talk to you about. I like the sound of your offer, and I'd love to go with it, but there's no way I'll be able to paint twenty paintings by October. The best I can probably do is December. Maybe January, but even that would be pushing it."

This is not good news.

I have no savings. I'm out of a job in a matter of weeks. I have loan repayments and maintenance bills due on the last day of each month.

Even if I do get Fleur on board, sell a few paintings that don't yet exist in advance for a December exhibition, that still leaves ... four months' worth of bills to pay with no income. And I know how hard it is to find a job these days after listening to the complaints of some of my friends.

I try to look on the bright side. At least she's *thinking* of signing with me. Which means my dream of owning a gallery isn't dead. It's just on hold for a while. I can always look for some other work in the meantime, even if it's nearly impossible to get hired in the current economy.

"Oh, that's okay," I tell her brightly. "That'll give us plenty of time to work the buyers into a bidding frenzy."

I'll figure something out.

I have to.

Maybe I can find another artist to exhibit in October. Some genius whose work is so good and so original, it'll sell like goddamn hotcakes and solve all my problems.

Sure.

"Grub's up," yells Nathan from another room.

I follow Fleur around the corner into a dining room.

And I stop dead in my tracks.

Holy fuck.

Paintings.

Unbelievably good paintings.

There are three of them. They're hanging on three different walls, each lit by a small spotlight, making the bold colors of the dramatic scenes jump out like 3D images. An electric jolt of excitement hits me right where it always does. In the middle of my chest, where my heartbeat kicks into an upbeat tempo.

Art is always the first thing I look for when I enter a room. It borders on addiction. So it's nothing unusual for me to stand and contemplate a painting I find. I always find myself considering its impact, its value and its influences.

But my reaction to these paintings is different. Instead of evaluating them, I'm being drawn into their magnetic intensity. I'm not thinking, I'm having a heartfelt emotional response. I *feel* them. Deeply.

I need these.

The three paintings look like they've been painted by the same artist, the style is similar enough. The first one is of a rampaging bull, the second one is of a horse, the third is of a beautiful dark-haired woman's face. The paintings' impact is visceral, attention-grabbing, forceful. These artworks are incredibly confident. And utterly original.

"Fleur," I manage to gasp. "Are these yours?" I know they're not hers. Even though I wish they were.

"No. No, they're not mine."

"Whose are they?"

"They're ... a local artist's. Who's not available, unfortunately."

I stare at her, still stunned. "Not available? Why not?"

The paintings are so alive, so colorful and intense, my head is spinning with the possibilities. These paintings will change the artist's life. Not to mention mine.

Nathan and Fleur are both looking at me, then they

glance at each other, with an indecisive expression, like they're grappling with a dilemma.

"Please." I'm ready to get down on my knees and beg. "Please tell me who painted these. They're incredible. It's such a difficult thing to do, to be completely free of comparison. I can't even see it: who are this artist's influences? There's nothing here except raw originality."

Fleur is quiet for a few seconds. Then she says, "What are you doing tomorrow, Ella?"

"I'm not sure. Why?"

"Tomorrow's the third and last day of the Bozeman Rodeo. Would you like to come with us to watch the show?"

I don't know why she's changing the subject. I get the feeling I've wandered into territory that needs to be handled carefully, even if I don't understand why. Maybe she's giving me a clue.

I can only hope.

I have no idea what a rodeo has to do with these paintings. And even though I've never been to a rodeo in my life and have no idea what to expect besides dust and farm animals and possibly even a cowboy or two, I hear myself saying, "I'd love to."

7

WILL

"*No*," I say again. "How many damn times do I have to say it, Fleur?" Then I instantly feel like shit. "I'm sorry. I didn't mean to swear at you. I meant to swear at him." I glare at Nathan. Nathan smiles but I don't smile back. The crowd is roaring, the sun is hotter than hell, I have a headache that won't quit and there's dust in my eyes. I can barely make out a flock of girls standing nearby, tittering and waving at me.

Fleur is relentless. "I know this probably isn't the best time to talk about this, Will, but I just thought—"

"Sweetheart. I've said it before and I'll say it again. I love you like a sister. Always have. But I'm very tempted to drive over to your house after I finish my ride and set fire to those paintings I gave you right there in your barbecue pit. Let's make a party out of it, in fact. You and Nathan can join me—if I'm still alive, that is—while I chug the hell out of a bottle of Jack until I'm passed out on the floor. Then you'll have nothing to hound me about and you can happily get on with your life."

"If you'd just give me a chance to *explain*, Will. There's someone I want to introduce you to—"

"Your timing sucks." I pull on my leather gloves. I'm seriously not in the mood for this shit.

I need to concentrate. I easily rode the full eight seconds yesterday and the day before that. But I still have one more ride to go.

"Later, then," insists Fleur.

"I'm busy later."

"I *really* think you'll want to hear this, Will."

"I don't. Now, if you'll excuse me, I've got a bull to ride."

Fleur can be irritatingly stubborn sometimes. She just will not quit. And she's still talking. "She's right here. It'll only take a second. Ella, this is Will. Will, Ella."

I notice her then, standing next to Fleur and Nathan. She's the same height as Fleur, and curvy but slim. Her hair is tied up but a few strands have come loose. It's a honey-colored dark blond and catches sunlight in hints of red and gold. Her olive skin is distractingly flawless, as though she might never have been sunburned in her life. She's wearing glasses like the ones you see in movies about city people trying to look trendy. Her clothes, too, make it obvious she's not from around here. She looks so out of her element it's almost comical. But she's cute, in a sassy, uptight kind of way. Like one of those hot librarians who, if you got her behind closed doors and stripped off her clothes and her rules, she'd morph into a submissively sex-crazed little wildcat.

The random thought gives me an instant, raging hard-on.

Fuck.

This is *not* what I need right now.

I don't bother exchanging niceties.

I storm away and climb up the fence to take my place as the headline act of the goddamn show. As usual, Jimmy Hogan's non-stop commentary splices straight through the middle of my concentration.

Can he continue his winning streak, ladies and gentlemen, or is Will Finn going to reacquaint himself with the hard ground and the crushing agony of defeat? Today he rides King Tut, the wily beast who unseated him six months ago, bringing pain and humiliation the likes which this champion had never seen!

Shit. I didn't realize *that* was the bull I'd be riding today. The same fucking one that almost killed me.

He's got to be feeling the nerves today, folks. He looks calm but underneath that stoic exterior his heart must be racing.

It is.

There's nothing else to do but ride the hell out of this fucker. I can't walk away. I'll face my challenge and, with any luck, come out on top.

Or I'll die trying.

I have a feeling, this time, it's one or the other.

"You got this," Luke says. "Easy as pie."

Sure. Easy as pie.

As I approach the bull, something strange happens. I start picturing my parents. Certain snapshot-like moments from my childhood. Christmas when I was seven and got a BB gun. Swimming in the river. Diving for gold nuggets that always turned out to be rocks. We didn't care. They were worth their weight in gold for all the fun they gave us.

My life is literally flashing before my eyes.

Maybe this is where it all comes to a screeching halt.

Maybe I'll never find out if the little librarian is a wildcat or not, I find myself thinking.

I climb onto King Tut, who snorts and paws the ground.

This is it, ladies and gentlemen. The ultimate show-down.

I feel surprisingly calm.

"Ready, Will?"

I grip the rope tight. "Ready."

The gate swings open and the bull bolts forward, leaping and twisting before it even hits the ground.

8

ELLA

NATHAN INSISTS that I leave my car at Fleur's and catch a ride with them in his monster truck. It's so high up, it affords a good view of, well, everything. The craggy mountain landscape, the endless blue sky and as we pull into the full parking lot, the rodeo.

It's packed. And here, as though the universe is finally delivering on its promise, are the answers to all my Kindle Unlimited prayers: cowboys. Thousands of them. Of all shapes and sizes. But, as I've now come to expect, the universe has a way of delivering a punchline. Because these aren't sweaty, muscular cowboys slinging hay bales. These are pudgy middle-Americans in cowboy hats eating fried dough.

Until we get closer to the ring.

And there ... *yes.* The chosen few. A cluster of handsome, muscle-bound, beefcake-type ones. They're all gathered around a fenced area next to a tall cage with an enormous bull in it. As we walk toward this beefcake brigade, things are really starting to look up, even though I'm still wondering why Fleur has brought me here. I forget about my question though, as I begin to get a better look. It's hard to see. The area is crowded. The sun is bright and dust is getting kicked up by the hot breeze and all the activity.

Nathan seamlessly becomes one with the beefcake brigade. Fleur, I can see, is talking to someone. My attention is momentarily diverted by the bull, who doesn't look at all happy to be in his cage. He (an educated guess) is snorting and stamping his feet. Fleur's talking to one of the beefcakes, who's being fussed over by some of the other people. They're giving him water and whiskey and pinning a competitor's number onto his back.

The crowd is cheering. I walk closer, behind Fleur. She's talking to the guy who I now understand is getting ready to ride the bull.

He's irritated. They're arguing.

And now that I get a better look at him—okay, *wow*. He looks like Nathan, only much, much better, if that's possible. A brother, very likely. He's absurdly handsome and manly and also mean-looking. Furious, almost. His hair is darker than Nathan's and he's bigger. Taller and more muscular. Like his alpha-ness is even more pronounced and somehow on steroids. The crowd is roaring, chanting something that sounds like *Will. Will. Will. Will.*

I catch the tail-end of their argument. "I don't," he says aggressively, to Fleur. "Now, if you'll excuse me, I've got a bull to ride."

His voice is husky, deep. And, weirdly, able to touch me in places I'm not sure I want to be touched. At least not right now while standing in the middle of this dusty rodeo arena.

He pulls on his leather gloves as Fleur says, "This is her, Will. Ella, this is Will. Will, Ella."

For a brief moment, he looks right at me. His expression remains hard as he takes in my wind-blown hair. I tied it up but strands have come loose. My glasses are smudged. My outfit, even though it seemed the height of Wild West fashion two days ago when I packed it, now feels totally out of place.

It's impossible not to notice the greenness of his eyes, which stun me with their ferocity, both of color and sheer, vibrant intensity. He's tall and wide-shouldered and built like a wall of muscle. A dark-haired, insanely *gorgeous* wall of muscle. We're talking movie star good looks. The kind that might be cast in a Brad Pitt movie. Or an erotica novella.

The rough, outrageous masculinity of him is ... well, a major freaking turn-on, if you really want to know. What I'm picturing is hot, dirty, take-no-prisoners sex. The kind that makes you see God and forget your own name. It would be like that with him, you can just tell that he'd fuck like a superhero.

Wow. Get a grip, girl.

Without a word, he stalks away, toward the bull pen. Despite his size, he moves with an animal grace and a self-assured arrogance that has everyone in the ring staring.

"Don't worry about him," Fleur says. "He's just a little distracted right now." She leads me up some stairs into the stands. I have a million questions. Who *is* he? Why did she invite me here? Is it possible that Mr. Rodeo McHottie is … ? No. It can't be.

The themes could be a fit. A bull. A horse. Who was the girl?

I want to ask Fleur, but it's too loud. The crowd is chanting. We take what appear to be VIP seats, close to the cage and Will, who is now climbing over the top of the bars.

He starts to ease himself down onto the bull until he's sitting astride its back.

Holy hell. That bull is *huge.*

The crowd roars, stomping and waving flags.

The announcer begins, with an almost macabre zeal.

Here he is, ladies and gentlemen, former state champion, taking only his third ride since his return. As we all know, six months ago, Will Finn suffered a bone-splintering fall that kept him out of the ring until two days ago, when he was the only competitor to ride a full eight seconds on the notorious King of

Spades. Yesterday, he again bested his brutal ride, General Lee. Has he used up all his luck, or can he pull off the trifecta?

The crowd goes wild, chanting Will's name.

This is King Tut, folks. The meanest, toughest bull in all Montana. The very bull that felled this rider, broke six of his ribs and sent him to the hospital by emergency ambulance. Not a single rider here today has bested this bull. If anyone can do it, it's Will Finn. But does he have the concentration? Or has he met his match yet again? To be trampled underfoot once more by this wily, feral two-ton beast will surely be the end of his career ... and quite possibly his life.

Jesus. I wish the announcer would stop his gruesomely descriptive play by play of the rider's accident. The poor guy, to be subjected to this cruel recap of something that must have been seriously traumatic for him. And to announce that his life is at risk right now? Who does that? But the announcer goes on, with the calm glee of a sado-masochist.

Hold onto your hats, ladies and gentlemen, and pray for this young hero's life.

My god. This is terrifying.

The crowd goes quiet.

The rider gives a signal. I stand up and I want to shout *wait!* But a horn sounds and the gate swings open. As soon as it does, the bull bolts forward, leaping and twisting.

Who would do this kind of thing for fun? If he falls off, *he could be killed!*

Why would someone so beautiful put himself at risk like this?

I feel light-headed with panic. I want him to *live*.

The bull surges left then jerks to the right. Somehow, Will is still holding on. His hand grips a rope strapped around the bull's chest. You can tell he's incredibly good at this, but the bull is bucking and writhing like a goddamn maniac.

Five seconds.

How many does he need? Eight? And then what happens?

Another twist. But Will is beginning to predict what the bull is going to do next. He's found a rhythm.

Six seconds.

The bull jumps forward, bucking to the left. Then the right.

Seven seconds.

The bull does a complete 180 in mid-air. Will's grip breaks and *I can't breathe*. He's thrown to the ground, hard, but somehow—a split second before the hooves of the bull land on his chest—he rolls away. Horns blare and people run forward to distract the bull and chase it into a tunnel under the stands.

My heart's racing.

I'm dizzy.

I feel like *I've* just ridden the bull.

He's done it, ladies and gentlemen! Eight point one five

seconds! Will Finn triumphs over King Tut but not without a painful reminder of exactly why this bull holds the record for unseating more riders than any other in Montana ...

Holy fuck.

AS SOON AS Will is safely out of the bull pen, he's swarmed by press and fans. He brushes past all of them, keeping his hat low on his head. Even in his black cowboy hat, his dirty double denim, his worn cowboy boots and a pair of dusty leather chaps, he looks more colorful than anyone else in the crowd. He's about a head taller than the swarm of people that are fighting for his attention, which he clearly has no interest in.

Fleur turns to me. "I'm sworn to secrecy," she says, "but in his own best interests, I'm asking you to guess why I brought you here."

"You want me to guess?"

"Yes. Guess." She's smiling and her eyes are a vivid shade of Montana blue.

"Is the artist of the paintings in your dining room here, somewhere, at the rodeo?"

"Good guess." She's pleased. "Keep guessing."

Is she suggesting ...? No, it's too outlandish a thought.

Sure, I would absolutely *love* for the ultra-hot rodeo hero to be The One. The artist who propels me to the top of the A-list art scene. Beefcake geniuses are even harder to come by than nerdy ones, I'm assuming. But it seems way too far-fetched, like an overly-optimistic plot twist of one of my cheesy romance novels. "Is it ..." I look around. There's a very round man who's around 5'2" standing nearby with a cowboy hat on, eating a corndog on a stick. "... him?"

Fleur gives me an exasperated look. "No. Guess again."

"Is he wearing a cowboy hat?"

"Yes."

"Chaps?"

"Yes."

"Double denim?"

"*Yes*, Ella."

I stare at Will from afar. He's taking a swig from a silver flask Nathan offers him. Then he walks through the crowd toward a red pick-up truck.

"Does he drive a red pick-up truck?"

"He sure does."

She's telling me what I want to hear, of course, but it still doesn't compute.

These things don't happen.

Especially not to me. I've serial-dated my way through the past seven years, with a string of duds, pricks, twits and assholes, each more mediocre in every conceivable cate-gory than the last. I'm twenty-five years old and have only had sex a handful of times, with each romp being so disappointing I'm beginning to wonder if there's something wrong with me. A man has never once given me an orgasm. Which is why I'm forced to resort to late-night sessions with my trusty vibrator and Kindle Unlimited subscription. Not that Will Finn has offered to change all that, of course. But still. The fact that he even *exists* seems like a sign that my luck is somehow on the up. "Are you suggesting the super-hot rodeo hero who just rode a very large bull for eight seconds is the same person who painted the masterpieces that are hanging in your dining room?"

Fleur smiles. "That's exactly what I'm suggesting."

Will peels out, leaving a cloud of chalky dust in his wake.

Montana dust has a flavor to it that stays with you. Like you've just become grittier and more salt-of-the-earth than you ever thought you could. I don't know why I say this but it tastes like the old, layered past mixed with the metallic gleam of the future and most of all the present, glittering with bright possibilities you'd never considered until now.

As soon as Will is gone, the scene seems strangely empty without him in it. Lacking in a particular excitement he'd unexpectedly infused into everything.

I feel—and this is unusual for me—momentarily speechless. Maybe some lucky star happened to glide into Jupiter's seventh house when I wasn't looking, who knows. What I *do* know is that this is simply too good to be true.

Except for one detail. He is, as Fleur put it … unavailable. "But why doesn't he want anyone to know? It doesn't make any sense."

"That's a question I can't answer," says Fleur. "It's just the way he is. I'll warn you now, he's as stubborn as an ornery mule and twice as bull-headed."

"I kind of got that impression."

"He's gruff, moody and temperamental as all get out," she adds. "And he's become sort of a hermit, which we were hoping was just part of his recovery. He used to be the life of the party."

That's okay, I find myself thinking. *He's ridiculously beautiful* and *he paints like a genius. No one's perfect. I'm not the life of the party, either.* "Artists often are." Am I defending him? I'm not sure.

"It'll be up to you to talk him around. I've already tried, and failed. Maybe he'll listen to you."

I have no idea why he would listen to me. I'm a total stranger who will clearly be invading his private world. Still, I feel my stubbornness kick in, behind my hesitations. *That kind of talent comes along once in a generation. It would be a crime to hide it away. I'll change his life for the better. It's worth taking a chance. Who knows, he might say yes.*

Or he might tell me right where to stick my fantasy gallery.

Nathan walks up to us. "We're heading to the house.

Luke and Casey are having a barbecue, to celebrate Will's win."

"Do you want to come, Ella?" Fleur's blue eyes glint in the sun. She's clearly trying to set me up with Will, or at the very least set up a meeting, which I appreciate, of course. I just get the feeling this is going to be anything but clear sailing.

"Thanks. I'd love to."

I climb up into the back seat of Nathan's black double-cab pick-up truck. Everyone around here drives the kind of vehicles that require bucketloads of testosterone to handle. As we're driving along, I feel the ping of my phone and pull it out of my pocket.

Did she sign or not?!?

James. I'd almost forgotten about him.

What to say? I decide to bluff and type a quick reply. I'm not having it out with James right now. If I pretend everything's on track, he'll give me more time.

Looking good. She's still considering it.

Which is true. Nothing has been signed.

Get the f#king deal DONE!!!*

Nice. I already consider myself out of a job. I don't want to continue working for that prick. And there's no way in hell I'd sign Fleur for James. I'll work harder for her. I'll give her the kind of exposure he never would.

If I can get my gallery up and running by December, that is.

If I can hit the ground running once I get back to New York and find whatever underling job I can get my hands on, to tide me over. I might not have to sell my dead mother's engagement ring. Or move out of the only home I've ever known. All I have to do is somehow hang on for four or five more months, at which point I'll schmooze some gullible bank loan officer into lending me a shitload of cash to secure the ideal and somehow still-affordable space I'll need to sell the hell out of Fleur's paintings to afford—which don't exist yet but will no doubt be brilliant enough to solve all my many financial problems.

Unless, of course ... I can get him. The sex god rodeo genius who's "unavailable."

In this moment, my plan feels wildly unrealistic. It's scary, and more than a little daunting.

Another text vibrates. *I'm counting on you, Ella. Get back to me ASAP!!!!!*

I turn off my phone and slide it into my pocket.

I glance out at the ridiculously scenic road to a lazy, rocky river whose water looks so clean I wish I could stop and drink it and swim in it and somehow be reborn as someone better than I am. Someone who had the guts to take the plunge a long time ago. Someone who'd been able to talk my parents into staying home on a rainy Tuesday night.

"Everything okay?" Fleur asks.

"Yes, fine," I say, sounding more upbeat than I feel.

"This is the Finns' ranch," she says.

We're driving under one of those rough-hewn home-made-style wooden archways you see in movies that serve as gateways into ... well, into Montana ranches. Every picture postcard of idyllic Montana scenery might have been taken right here. The grass is a surreal shade of neon-green, the ice-blue river water sparkles like jewels and the blue sky is a bright, clear azure expanse that somehow seems twice as big as the skies of New York. There aren't even any white trails of planes, like you always see in the city. And not a molecule of smog. The only clues that humankind even exists beyond Nathan's truck are the tall, sturdy-looking wooden fences that stretch as far as the eye can see.

"It's so beautiful," I say, stating the obvious, but I can't help it. It really is.

We drive another ten minutes or so until we can see the house, which is a huge, rustic, awesome log-cabin type mansion that's made of actual logs and stone. The logs look they they've been sawed down complete, dragged by teams of mules and stacked by hand. Six or seven other pick-up trucks are already parked in the driveway. No red ones, though. There are people gathered on the massive porch, which runs the entire length of the house and wraps around it.

Nathan parks on the grass. I walk with them up to the "homestead," they call it, and Fleur starts introducing me.

"Ella, this is Luke, Nathan and Will's older brother. And this is Casey, his wife."

"Hi, Ella."

Luke is tall and has dark blond hair, even darker blond sideburns and strapping, down-home good looks. Casey's hair is wavy and brown. She has bright blue eyes and a freckled, sun-kissed face. If I had to judge them on looks alone I'd say they were the most wholesome, healthy people I've ever met. They radiate a relaxed, genuine happiness that makes me want to bask in their glow. I'm not sure why, but I envy them.

I learn that Luke and Casey and their baby son, Wade, live in the big house. There are seven spare bedrooms. Nathan lives with Fleur, and Will lives in another cabin nearby, down by the river. Another brother named Jack lives with Will some of the time, or at the homestead. And the youngest brother, Wyatt, also lives at the homestead but they hardly ever see him since sleeps his way around the community. All five brothers work on the ranch. They all have done or do rodeo, but Will's the best.

Of all the brothers, only Luke and Nathan are at the party and I can't help wondering if Will might be coming. Fleur takes me aside, to the edge of the porch, where we lean against the wide log railings and look out to the river in the distance. The sun is lower in the sky now and is beginning to paint the horizon with the first orange hues of sunset.

"I just got a call from Amanda Riggs at the Blackbird," Fleur says. "She said Roxanne Mayberry wants meet with me tonight. I had promised her a meeting and it turns out she's heading back to New York early tomorrow morning."

This isn't great news, only because I'm sort of relying on Fleur to be my guide, and to help me navigate this whole Will situation. And even though I know there's a snowball's chance in hell that Roxanne will match the prices I've offered Fleur, no contract has been signed yet.

As always, Nathan is close by. "This Roxanne is saying your boss would never offer the prices you're offering." Nathan would probably do well in New York if he ever decides to go there. He's unflinching direct.

And so am I. "That's because he's not offering them. I am."

"But how can you guarantee those prices if you don't even have any real estate yet?" Nathan says, spearing straight to the heart of all my inadequacies. "What if it doesn't happen the way you say it will?"

It's a good question, unfortunately. Luckily, I've been stewing about that very topic non-stop, so I'm able to give him an answer. "I don't have any real estate—yet—but I do have a track record. I guarantee I'll deliver what I've promised, and if I can't, we'll write it into the contract that Fleur will be free to take her paintings else-where. So she can't lose, either way." *Plus she can have my first-born child,* I feel like saying, but don't. If I lose Fleur,

I'll be back to square one. Or square zero, more accurately.

Fleur puts her hand on my shoulder. "I believe you'll get what you say, Ella, and I'm definitely leaning toward signing with you. But I did promise her a meeting. I'd be crazy not to just listen to Roxanne and see what she's offering. Nathan thinks I should and I agree."

"Of course. You should take your time and think everything through."

"Casey wants you to stay in one of the spare rooms here tonight," Fleur says. "It's already arranged. Nathan and I might be late by the time the meeting is over. We'll come pick you up tomorrow morning. Nathan's already put your bag by the stairs. You've got my number. I'll call Will now and see if I can get him to come up here to talk with you."

"Now?"

"Yes."

God. Am I ready for a showdown with Will Finn? Yes, of course I am. I have to be. I have a very limited amount of time to convince him I'm the answer to all his unwanted prayers.

Fleur finds his number and puts her phone on speaker.

It rings five times and by the fifth ring I'm almost hoping he doesn't pick up.

"Yeah?" His voice has a deep, soft husk to it.

"Hey, Will."

"Hey, Fleur."

"That was some ride. You okay?"

"Fine."

"That fall looked like it hurt."

"It would've if the bull had landed two inches to the left."

"Yeah. Well, I'm glad you're okay."

As though she's trying his endless patience by bothering him: "What do you need?"

"Are you coming up to the house?"

"No."

Fleur sighs. "You should, Will. Come up."

Silence.

"There's someone here I think you might like to talk to. Her name is Ella."

"The one who was with you today?" *Of course I remember our one second of sizzling eye contact. And so does he.*

"Yes," says Fleur. "Ella Parker. She's from New York."

More silence.

"It won't take long, Will. You can just–"

"No, Fleur. I'm hanging up now. You can tell Ella Parker she can get that hot little librarian ass back to New York where it belongs."

What? Did he just say what I think he just said?

"Will, it's important. I *really* think you'll want to hear this."

The line goes quiet. I wonder for a second if he's hung up.

"Will?"

His tone is different when he continues. Still low and husked, but with an annoyed, provoked edge. I get the distinct feeling this is a sore point between the two of them. I also get the feeling he doesn't realize he's on speakerphone. "Fleur, I'm seriously not in the mood for this shit. If you don't drop all this—as I think I've already mentioned, more than once—I'm going to drive over to your house and take those paintings I gave you, which I'm now severely regretting. I'm going to bring them back here and burn them with all the rest of the ones I have in the biggest bonfire Montana's ever seen. You'll see the smoke. In fact, I might go get them now."

"Will—"

"I said drop it, okay?"

Some small ache in my chest almost feels like heartbreak. He doesn't sound very negotiable. At all. But I can take one glimmer of hope from his rant. *He has more paintings.* If he's going to create the biggest bonfire Montana has ever seen, he might have ... *a lot* more paintings.

"Will," says Fleur, "do you remember when I pulled Baxter out of the river when we were seven years old?"

Baxter? Who's Baxter?

More silence.

"Will?"

"Yes."

"You said to me then that if there was anything you could ever do for me, just name it, and you would."

"Fucking hell, Fleur." Will sounds exasperated. "You're really going to play the Baxter card right now?"

"Yes. It's *that* important to me. I'm absolutely playing it."

"He's still the best dog I ever had." He sounds nostalgic.

"Exactly," says Fleur. "*Baxter* would want you to talk to Ella, if he was still with us. We *all* want you to talk to Ella. Because we care about you and she might just change your life."

Wow, this conversation is getting heavy.

Will sighs heavily. But he doesn't refuse.

"So you'll agree to it?" Fleur, I'm learning, is a lot like me. Sort of relentless. In a good way.

"*Fuck.* I can't believe this."

Fleur beams at me and Nathan is shaking his head, laughing lightly, like he understands only too well how good she is at getting her way.

"Tell her she can come down here," Will says. "I'll give her five minutes."

"Great. Thank you, Will. I'm sending her down there now. Just listen to what she has to say. Then we're even."

"We sure the hell are."

The line goes dead.

9

—————

WILL

I should never have answered my damn phone.

I end the call, turn my phone off and take another swig of whiskey. That's what I'm going to do tonight: get wasted. Maybe later I'll paint a picture.

It would be easy enough to go out for a while. To disappear. Or lock my door.

But I can't. She played the goddamn Baxter card. Which means I can't get out of this. We had a pact all those years ago.

It'll be a waste of time, for this *Ella Parker*. And for me. But I have no choice.

Now that I think about it, I should have gone up to the house to meet with her. Then at least I could leave after the five minutes are up.

I consider it, as I sit here watching the sunlight dance across the glittering surface of the river. I start to get up.

But then I see a small figure appear on the horizon. Making her way down the dirt road toward my house. In her fucking high heeled boots. It's slow going. She's trying to avoid the grooves in the track and her heels keep sinking into the soft mud.

It would be hilarious if I had a sense of humor right now. Which I don't. But there's something mildly entertaining about watching her. She's so resolute. She's going to get down here or die trying, you can just tell. And something about the combination of her awkwardness and her sassy little stride is getting me all fucking worked up, go figure.

I can see her face now. The determined expression. The tied-up dark-blond hair and those city glasses. The pouting pink mouth.

Her clothes are fitted. Suede pants and an off-white shirt. Both hug her body in a way that reminds me of my first reaction to her. I feel it happening again, even though I don't particularly *want* to react to her this way. The last thing I need is to be lusting after an uptight city girl. More likely I'm just feeling the effects of being out of the saddle for seven entire months. An all-time record. Then again, at least she's not a rodeo groupie. I won't bump into her on the circuit and feel obliged to make small talk.

After the ten minutes it takes her to walk down the hill, she arrives at the foot of the steps of my porch. More strands of her hair have come loose. Her boots are muddy and her clothes are dusty. She looks up at me and adjusts her smeared glasses.

My hat is down low over my eyes and I raise my head enough to glare at her from under the rim. She blushes a little and smooths her clothes self-consciously. I didn't fully appreciate it at the rodeo but she really does have a killer little body under all those hoity-toity clothes.

Good thing I'm still wearing my leather chaps, which might partly hide how rock hard and gargantuan my cock has become. Then again, who cares if she notices? The sight of my enraged hard-on might be enough to unsettle her and spook her back on up the road.

"Mr. Finn?"

This almost makes me smile. Seriously?

I don't answer her right away. I want to watch her squirm.

"Mr. Finn, I was wondering if we could talk. I'm—"

"Ella Parker. I know. I heard you were coming."

"I'm sorry to barge in on you like this, but I really wanted to talk to you about—"

"Come on up." I could tell her to fuck off, which is what common sense is telling me to do. But as pissed off as I may be, I still have manners, like it or not. My father ingrained us with that shit from a young age, and on the odd occasion it didn't take, he'd beat it into us.

I have no idea why, but I want to fluster her.

She makes her way nimbly up the steps and as she gets

closer, I again notice the flawlessness of her skin. Even with her face hidden behind those city glasses, she really is sort of … stunningly pretty.

"Want a whiskey?" I ask her.

"I, um … I guess I—"

"Take a seat." I grab one of the tin cups that are on the table and wipe it with my shirt before pouring a double shot of Jack into it. I offer it to her as she sits.

"Thanks."

I'm holding it out to her but she doesn't immediately take it. Like she's scared of it. Then she slides two delicate-looking fingers through the handle of the mug. She takes the smallest sip you could possibly take and coughs a little, then blushes as she glances over at me. I notice then that her eyes are the color of warm brandy, a golden color with paler, light-catching flecks. Her eyes and her hair match perfectly.

She's clearly about three thousand miles out of her comfort zone and this amuses me, even though I don't let on.

The universe does occasionally give you what you've been looking for when you think about it often enough and crave it hard enough. The curve of her mouth, the shape of her face and the outrageous lines of her sweet little body have given me an idea.

10

ELLA

SOMEHOW I MAKE it down the death-defying dirt track without falling into one of the Grand Canyon-style potholes, to this to-die-for modern log cabin surrounded by green pastures and rocky mountains, which is just about the most picturesque place I've ever seen. And now Mr. Sex God Rodeo is sitting there, all cool and borderline asshole-ish—which I can almost understand, since I just bowled up to his front porch only after he was coerced into agreeing to meet with me because of some long-ago pact made over the rescue of his beloved childhood doggie.

This whole thing is ... intimidating. I don't know exactly how to begin.

But there's no time for weakness. Or weak-kneed, star struck adoration. I'm here to pitch a business proposal that could make us both rich. I need to keep my eye on the ball.

Not on that crazy-thick black hair, that curls out in

loose flicks from under his hat. Or those striking green eyes rimmed with dense lashes that are glaring at me.

Or that sinfully-perfect mouth that's almost sneering.

Or that jaw and neck and shoulders that have clearly slung their fair share of hay bales and which could also be featured in some guidebook about over-the-top specimens of A-list masculinity the likes of which this New Yorker has never seen.

Or those cowboy boots. Like, *real* cowboy boots. As opposed to the kind I'm wearing, which are now beyond hope and coated ankle-deep in mud.

Or those ridiculously muscular thighs.

Or that incredibly large ... *swell ... oh, Jesus.*

I can't handle this.

Yes, you can. Cowgirl up, Ella Parker, and get what you came for.

Or get a lot more *than you came for.*

He's mind-numbingly gorgeous. It's a level of hotness that awes you and stuns you with the sheer force of it.

I want to touch him. I want to lick *him, to see what he tastes like. I want to do things with Will Finn I've never done. I want to get naked with him and drive him wild with hot, feral lust.*

Holy hell.

He's still glaring at me.

And I need to concentrate on what's at stake here.

So, after he invites me, I walk up the steps and carefully sit in the chair he's sort of offering me. It looks like it might have been carved by someone who … carves stuff. With an actual knife. It looks like the kind of thing you could get splinters from, but I try to ignore this detail. I mean, if Will Finn can get thrown off an angry two-ton bull, almost get stomped on and hardly flinch, I'm sure I can handle a splinter or two.

I take a sip of my (very generously poured) cup of whiskey. Served in one of those tin mugs you see movie cowboys drink out of when they're sitting around the campfire playing their harmonicas. In actual fact, I've never drunk whiskey before in my life and it's basically like drinking liquid fire. It burns all the way down my throat and I try not to cough, but I can't help it.

He's watching me and he's got this arrogant, almost-amused look on his face, like something about me is mildly funny to him. "All right?" he says.

"Fine, thanks." I smile and try to sound casual. I take another sip of whiskey just to prove to him that I can drink it without coughing. Which I do. But my eyes water.

I notice as I look out at the landscape while I drink a little more of the whiskey (it grows on you once you get used to it) that the sun is starting to go down. I'm not looking forward to navigating those big-ass muddy potholes in the dark so I guess I better get down to business.

"So, Mr. Finn," I begin, but before I can, he starts

laughing. And hell, if I thought he was good-looking when he was grumpy, *damn*. The sight of his smile and the sound of his deep, relaxed man-laughter makes something in me melt a little. Okay, more than melt. Break. Or fall. There's no verb that accurately sums it up. Because I'm sitting here drinking whiskey with a real live cowboy who's not only gorgeous in a way that's beyond the scope of any kind of gorgeousness I've ever expected to actually see in this lifetime, he's also—not to be overly dramatic—the answer to all my fantasies, prayers, goals and aspirations.

And he's laughing.

"It's Will," he says, still smiling. "Just call me Will."

"Oh. Okay. Well, um, *Will*, the reason I'm here is that I, well, I was over at Fleur's house, and, uh ..." This is surprisingly difficult to bring up, is what it boils down to. Because I don't want to make him angry again. And I have a feeling this is going to. But the sun is setting. I think of my bills coming up at the end of the month and my employment contract that's about to expire. And I say it anyway. "I saw a few of your paintings at Fleur's house and I was wondering if you have any more. And if you'd like to exhibit them. With me. At my new gallery. I'd like to make you an offer you can't refuse."

He looks out over his panoramic view of the hills and the river and his smile almost lingers, but not quite. "Oh, I can refuse it."

Um. Okay, Ella, now what?

Say something convincing. Something fun and unexpected that might begin to change his mind.

"Of course you *can* refuse it," I reply jauntily. "But you won't *want* to, as soon as you hear more about what it is I'm about to tell you."

His gaze moves lazily across the landscape, like he's not in a hurry. Then it finally lands on me. But he says nothing, making me flush again under his unwavering glare.

I do my best not to wither in the face of his scorn and indifference. "I was wondering if you have any other paintings. Besides the ones at Fleur's."

We both watch the last sliver of the sun disappear over the mountains. He tips back the rest of his whiskey. "Mmhm."

"Mmhm? Does that mean ... yes?"

"Yes."

"You *do*?"

"I do."

Thank you, universe. Thank you, Kindle Unlimited. Thank you, Fleur. This is exceptionally fabulous news. "How *many* ... would you say you ... might have?"

More silence. Then, finally, "Probably around two fifty or three hundred. Maybe more."

"Two *hundred* and fifty?" Jesus. That's ten freaking exhibitions' worth and then some.

"Give or take."

I glance through the screen door of his cabin, longingly.

"But I'm not interested in exhibiting them. At all. Ever. It's just something I do when I'm alone and I plan on keeping it that way."

I'm not sure if it's obvious to him that he's just speared through my heart with a metaphorical bloody sword, all the way to the hilt. But I'd been warned to expect some bull-headedness, and I geared up for it all the way down the muddy trail. "But, Mr.—*Will* ... I really think you should reconsider!" (I try not to add the exclamation point but it ekes out.) "Please, just hear me out. See, I'm in the process of starting up a new gallery in New York City, in SoHo, and it's going to be *the* place to exhibit. Fleur's going to exhibit with me in December—well, I mean, I *hope* she will and she's definitely seriously considering it. Her work will get her huge visibility. And it'll also make her a lot of money. A *lot* of money." I feel foolish for repeating it. "I have an open window for October and I'm looking for the perfect artist. You, Will ... you're perfect." That would be the understatement of the millennium.

He doesn't seem impressed, but I'm used to artists being wary of the first offer they're given.

So I keep going. "Fleur's paintings are amazing. But yours are, like, *once-in-a-lifetime* good. Yours are exceptional. You know that, right? Do you know how good you are?"

"I'm not interested."

I stare at him. The way he said that was so final-sounding. "You're not interested in money?"

"I have enough money."

I blink once. Twice. "Can anyone really ever have enough money?"

"Yes." He grabs the bottle of whiskey and takes a swig directly out of it, contemplating the view, which is now a dark purple mountain range and a big orange sky with a glowing neon line that runs the length of the craggy horizon. The river glows orange with the reflection of it all. A few stars are already out. It really is breath-taking. "Look at my view," he says. "My house. My truck. My motorcycle. I have twelve horses, five dogs, six hunting rifles, I personally own four hundred head of cattle, I have a seventy-inch flat screen, a killer stereo system and as much whiskey as a man could ever drink. What else do I need?"

I've never once had anyone ask me that question before. "Um ... a Maserati?"

He raises one perfect eyebrow. "Have you seen those potholes? It would fall in."

"True. How about world travel?"

"Never really had the urge. I like Montana."

"You've never wanted to go to, say, Rome?"

"Not really."

"To see the Sistine Chapel ceiling?"

"I could do that now if I wanted to."

He really is very stubborn. "Maybe some gold necklaces?"

This makes him smile. His teeth are square and white. The shape of his mouth is having a strange effect on me. You can just tell from the smile and the sneer that he'd be dirty and aggressive. That he'd take you places you've never, ever been.

I rub my palm on the arm of my chair, almost hoping for a splinter. I want to *feel* something. A little bite of pain. To ground me. To keep me from doing something I might regret.

As if you'd regret a single second of it.

Will puts his feet up on the porch railing and leans back in his chair. His hat slips back a fraction. From the warm light pouring out from lamps inside the windows of his house, I can see that his thick black hair is sticking out from under the rim of his hat. I find myself wondering what grabbing handfuls of the coarse silk of it would feel like. "The answer is no."

"You could quit rodeo, and not have to risk your life anymore."

"I don't do rodeo for the money. I do it for the rush. The thrill. The win."

"But it's so dangerous."

"A little danger is good for the soul. Have you ever experienced danger, Ella Parker?" He's watching me as he says my name and at this point I might be a puddle on the rough-hewn wooden floor, it's hard to tell. He's just so insanely good-looking. And *big. ALPHA* is written all over him. His outrageous ruggedness is making me feel restless. And hot. *And wet. Goddamn it.*

He's even making my fictional book boyfriends seem lame and that's saying something.

Calm down, girl. Yes, he's hot. Yes, he's talented. He's also arrogant AF and is currently in the process of telling you he's not interested in anything you have to offer.

"I almost fell into several mammoth potholes on my way down here," I say. "If that isn't danger, I don't know what is." I almost mention that, even with my flashlight app, the thought of mincing my way back up the trail in the dark is more than a little scary. But maybe he's right. Maybe a little danger *is* good for the soul. Anyway, I've got nothing to lose at this point. "So, for your first exhibition—if you happen to change your mind—you'd be looking to make around one point four million dollars."

I let the amount hang there in the ludicrously fresh air for a few seconds. He doesn't say anything. A dog trots up the steps and starts sniffing me and whacking me with its muscular tail. "Come here, Pearl," he says softly. Pearl obeys, licks his hand a few times, then lays at his feet with a loud, contented sigh.

I wait for Will to react to what I've just told him. He doesn't, aside from taking another sip from his bottle of Jack. He must have a strong tolerance because I'm half surprised he's not wasted by this point, because I'm already feeling my buzz. Then again, he probably weighs twice what I weigh and then some.

"People would be intrigued by your art, because it's original," I tell him. "But they'd also be intrigued by your story. People love a story." I can imagine the headlines now: *Smokin' Hot Rodeo Hero Paints Like a Genius*.

"You've already done the math?" he says. "Isn't that counting your chickens just a little early?"

Chickens?

"I don't have much use for one point four million dollars," he drawls. "As I said, I have enough money, enough land, enough—"

"Dogs and horses, yes, I heard. I just think you should take a little time to consider what I'm offering you. Your paintings are extraordinary. You're an incredible talent. You'd be a sensation. Your work deserves to be seen, by people who know how good you are. People who would value your talent more than you can imagine."

"What 'people' are these?" he says, sounding bored.

Focus, Ella, I scold myself. I adjust my glasses, which are so streaked and dusty I can hardly see out of them. "Um, well, like art dealers. Buyers. Collectors. Museum curators. Magazine editors. Art writers. Critics."

"Critics?" Will sneers. "Why would I want critics analyzing my art?"

"People who pay a lot of money for art often have one

or two knowledgeable critics they trust to compare the artist's work to other artists, and that can help determine the value of a piece."

"Shit," he chuckles. "Why should I care what some twit critic thinks my art is worth?"

"Um, because that's how you make *money* out of it. Lots of money, if they think it's worth it. Which they will. Because it is."

"It doesn't matter. Because I don't want to show them. It stays where it is."

I'm speechless, which is rare. I never imagined anyone could be so obstinate.

I can feel my gallery slipping through my fingers.

But then, after a long pause, Will says, "There's one way I'd consider showing you."

There is? I perk up immediately. It takes every ounce of willpower I possess, but I wait for him to continue.

"The paintings are upstairs in my loft."

"Oh."

"There's something I need. Which you could ... provide."

I glare at him warily. Is he propositioning me? Would I mind? *Of course you wouldn't mind, you idiot! Admit it: you'd do any damn thing Will Finn asked you to. Right now.* "What thing?"

"I doubt you'll agree to it."

I'm not sure why I ask it, but I just want to make sure. "Does it have to do with ... rodeo?"

He laughs. A real laugh. His laughter is musical and genuine and so damn manly I feel myself ... *oh no*. I'm drowning in his pheromones. My panties get even wetter. I feel soft and warm. My nipples bud into tight peaks. I can feel my heartbeat *everywhere*.

"No," he confirms. "Although you could probably *talk* a bull into submission."

I'm not sure how to respond to that. Because my body is reacting to the sound of his rough, deep voice. I need to get a grip. I can't get carried away by this sexy cowboy who might—just might—make all my wildest dreams come true. "What's the thing you need, then?"

"I've been wanting to do a new series," he says, watching my face.

"Oh."

"You can only paint a cow so many times. Or a bull. Or a horse. Or a mountain."

"What kind of series are you thinking of?"

"You. I need a model."

I DO what any sane person would do. I laugh. "God, no. I don't think I'm the right person for that. I'm sure any one of those girls today at the rodeo would be lining up to be your model. I'm a curator, not a model."

He's watching me. I feel myself blush, which is weird. I'm not a person who blushes easily. Or at least I wasn't until five minutes ago. But he's checking me out, like he's already thinking about how he might paint me.

"I don't want them," Will says, making things worse. "I want you."

I'll admit I'm having a major moment of weakness. *He's a genius. And he wants to paint* me. *I'd be crazy not to go with this.*

But— "Would I have to …?" I mean, does he want, like, a *nude* model?

"Not unless you want to." He's smiling, and it's sort of heart-breaking. *He* could be a model, if GQ scouts traveled this far out. "You can keep your clothes on."

"Who was the woman in the painting at Fleur's?" I ask, before I can stop myself. It was just her face, sort of haunting and peaceful, with strands of her dark hair caught by the breeze.

"My mother. From a photo. It didn't do her justice. She was much more beautiful than that in my memory."

Was. "I'm sorry."

He doesn't say anything else on that topic and the silence isn't silent at all. There are cows mooing in the distance and the rush of the river water is more soothing than white noise (the only way I've ever actually heard river sounds, come to think of it). "I lost my parents when I was sixteen," I hear myself say. "In a car crash."

Will's eyes are a vivid, intensity-filled shade of green, even in the dark, and are sparked with deep, vibrant intelligence. You can tell he's got something other people don't, just by looking into his eyes. "I was seventeen when I lost mine. A cattle truck, fully loaded, hit them head-on."

So we have two things in common.

We're quiet for a while, but he clinks his whiskey bottle against my tin cup and we drink to the memory of our dead parents, which has suddenly become sort of emotional, even though it was a long time ago. Maybe the two fingers of whiskey I've already sipped my way through are starting to have their way with me.

He barely nods toward the door. "So what do you say?"

I'm not going to refuse him, of course I'm not. We've just shared a moment that was surprisingly heavy. Plus, *he's going to show me his paintings.*

But ... I think I might have just agreed to be his model.

WILL STANDS up and I notice again by how big he is. How freaking *built.* I take off my muddy boots before following him into his cabin so I don't track half of Montana in with me. He tosses his cowboy hat onto a couch. Even with his hair still stuck in place from his hat, there's something ridiculously appealing about it. It's black and thick, with a wave to it. He unbuckles his suede chaps and tosses them onto a chair and I get a brief look at ... the ludicrously perfect way his jeans fit his spectacularly buff, toned body *(that ass, holy hell)*—and also the living room, which is open plan and amazing and very much a bachelor pad, with saddles and lassos and cowboy hats and dogs sort of artfully strewn around. Will heads straight up the stairs, taking three of them with each step, to a door at the top.

He glances back to make sure I'm following him.

I am, but I'm nervous. *Can I handle this?*

You have to handle it, buttercup. Get your sweet ass up those stairs and do whatever this hot, brooding rodeo hero tells you to.

I make my way up the stairs and hesitate for only a second before walking through the door of his studio. Something about entering his domain feels invasive, even though he's inviting me in. Like I'm not just entering a room but walking through a portal through a space-time continuum that I know for sure will change my life.

Subdued lamplight illuminates the large space. His loft must take up the entire second story of the house.

And it's filled to bursting with art.

I can hardly breathe.

Paintings are perched on a dozen or more easels around the room and stacked in rows of fives and tens against the walls, which are covered in many, many more of them. Paintings and drawings and doodles on paper cover every inch of the wood-beam walls. Quotes and ripped out magazine articles and photos are everywhere. Tables and shelves are filled with books, trinkets, paintbrushes and tube after tube of paint. It's the organized chaos of a mind bursting with ideas.

Water jars are full of paint brushes. At least ten paint-stained palettes are scattered throughout the room. An oversized worn leather couch and two cowboy-sized leather chairs sit facing a huge window, and I can see the full moon and what looks like the entire Milky Way, splashed brightly across the sky. There's a cluttered wooden coffee table in front of the couch. A large bed at the far end of the room under another window is unmade.

I can only stare. Already I can see several series. There are some that fit with the rampaging bull at Fleur's. There's a series of horses. One of landscapes. There are allegorical scenes of people and symbols, painted in bold colors and expressive black lines. Twenty or thirty colorful spiral paintings leap off their canvases.

Sweet Jesus.

These are better than the paintings at Fleur's. Even more striking and emotionally intense.

"These are so *good*, Will," I manage to say. I sound breathless, and no wonder. "Do you know how *good* you are?"

"It doesn't matter." Will leans his shoulder against the wall and folds his brawny arms, watching me.

"Of course it matters."

I'm awestruck, again, by how ridiculously handsome he is. And sort of aggressive-looking.

But I'm too distracted to worry about how beefy and powerful Will Finn is. All I can think about is how powerful his art is.

He lets me look. I wander carefully through the clutter. I don't touch anything—it feels too soon—but I don't need to. It's masterpiece after masterpiece. It's the kind of art that shakes up a scene and changes everything.

I'm so awestruck it takes me a minute to realize he's setting up an easel. He's squeezing some paint onto one of his palettes. He's choosing a paintbrush.

That was the deal. He lets me see his art and I let him paint me.

It's awkward, almost. But then he pulls his shirt over his head and tosses it aside, like he's getting comfortable before he gets into his groove, and—*holy fuck*. I forget how awkward I feel, and everything else. My brain is so full of the vision of him and his sculpted, hair-dusted masculine AF body, no other thoughts will fit in there.

It's overwhelming, this overload of him and his rodeo drama, the journey to get here, the art, and now his beefed-up glory that's around a million times more spectacular than anything I imagined in my Kindle fantasies.

Because it's *real* and I'm locked away with it here in this room approximately three thousand miles from anything even remotely familiar to me.

I'm staring. He's not just buff, he's *ripped*. His shoulders and chest are broad and sculpted and muscular as all get out, tapering down to the kind of quilted washboard abs "washboard abs" were named after. His Levi's are worn-in and dirty and hanging low on his hips in a way that's blowing my mind a little, if you really want to know. He's got that V thing going on, which fascinates me to no end. All that, combined with the arrogance and the face and the hair and the rimmed green eyes ... *someone help me. I'm in way over my head here.*

He's quite literally to-die-for, and it's tilting my entire life off its axis because I know for a fact that no one will ever be able to beat this. This moment means something. It's a benchmark that's now etched irrevocably into my brain. Every time I go on a bad date (and they always are) or wish the conversation wasn't so insipid or that the person on the other side of the table was just a little more on my wavelength, *this* is what I'll be thinking of.

No one should be this perfect, damn him.

It's not fair. It's going to make me agree to *do* things, I can just tell. It's going to make me *want* to do things. All kinds of things. Starting with taking off my top layer. It's sweltering up here, first of all. Second, he took off his shirt, so it feels like I should get even. I don't want to be all dressed up like a nun on vacation when he's all free and easy with his pair of jeans on and nothing else. *A pair of jeans he just so happens to be filling out like nobody's business.*

So he's not just dreamy and talented beyond belief.

He's also hung like a freaking porn star.

Ella, I scold myself. *It's shallow to fixate on details like that.*

I'm wearing a white tank top over a lacy white bra and my light faux-suede pants (which almost seem foolish after the thick *real*ness of his chaps, but whatever). I lean against the arm of the massive leather couch, uneasily. I don't know the first thing about how to be a model.

He seems to read my discomfort. "I'm sorry if this is a strange request. Painting you, I mean. It's just that I've been thinking about it a lot lately. And I don't have anyone to paint."

"What about one of the women who were at the rodeo today?"

"They're only interested in one thing."

"Oh." Sometimes I wish I was the kind of person who could refrain from asking the thoughts that pop into my head ... but, "And you're not?"

Will gives me a hot, smoldering look that basically has the exact same effect as mainlining an uncut aphrodisiac. *Damn it.* The alpha pheromones he's emitting are hitting my system big time. I'm dizzyingly aware of the way my nipples have beaded into tight little peaks. I can feel my warm pulse in a *very* intimate place and it's distracting.

"I've been looking for a certain ... something," he says, "that none of them have."

"Oh." Wow. "And I do?"

"Yes."

I think he might have just given me a compliment. "What's ... the certain something?"

"A look."

"What kind of look?"

"The look of a perfect stranger."

I'm not sure how to read this. Maybe he doesn't want to paint anyone he knows.

"Take a seat on the couch, if you want." Will's gaze wanders across my face and my body like he's getting a feel for the outlines of me. His eyes are intense and this suddenly feels sort of ... intimate.

I sit, sort of gingerly, because all my senses are on overdrive and it's disorienting me, on the edge of the couch.

Then he does something I'm not expecting. He walks over to me. He leans over me. My breath catches. He carefully touches his rough fingers to my face, adjusting the tilt of my chin.

He's touching me. And dazzling me on about ten different levels.

I literally swoon and it's a good thing I'm almost sitting down.

His strong hand catches hold of my arm, to steady me. "Whoa." He does that not-quite-smiling thing again. "All right?"

"Fine," I say, even though I'm not fine. Not at all. I'm high on life. I'm woozy from being this close to him. The scent of him is a heady mixture of leather and rodeo dust and sunshine.

He helps me sit on his huge couch. "Sit back and get comfortable. I'm just going to paint your face, to start with."

I lay back a little further. "Go ahead."

He goes back to his easel and pulls up a tall wooden stool. He adjusts the canvas. "That's good," he says. "I want to get that crazy light in your eyes."

Will starts painting.

The couch is comfortable. The view isn't bad either.

If someone ever asked me to describe a scene that might make my life complete, I would have struggled to come up with one as flawless as this. Loosely, he holds his palette in his left hand. He dips his brush into the paint and glides it onto the canvas, which I can't see from this angle. His movements are so confident, so sure.

I wish *I* could be that sure. About anything at all.

I watch him. His thick, too-long hair, a glorious mess. His manly, to-die-for face with its square jaw and the shadow of his stubble. The vivid color of his eyes as he paints me. The graceful movement of his muscular, sun-bronzed shoulders. I take in every detail, and my brain struggles to calibrate the magnificence, the long list of things to marvel at. I can admit that I'm falling deeper and deeper into my enchantment. It's justified, I figure.

"So how'd you get into the art scene?" he says. Maybe he's trying to put me at ease, to break the silence.

"I've always been an art appreciator, I guess you could say. My mother painted. But my father couldn't draw a stick figure to save his life. Like me."

"You don't paint?"

"No. Not at all. I've always loved looking at art, though. My father did too. Every Saturday when I was young, we'd leave my mother at home to paint her commissions and my father and I would go to the galleries and the new exhibitions around the city. We'd talk about which ones stood out from the rest. We'd try to figure out who the artists' influences were and so on. It was our thing. By the time I was twelve, my father said I knew more than most of the critics and art writers. And I could predict which of the up-and-coming artists would make a splash. I had a knack for it, he said. I was obsessed, partly because I wanted to please him, but then it sort of became a part of my outlook, and I ended up getting an Art History degree and a job." I laugh weakly. I'd forgotten some of the details of those particular memories. The way I'd hold onto my father's hand as we walked through the Met, or how we once got locked inside the Guggenheim without the guards realizing it because we stayed so late. We'd talk about one day owning our own gallery. It was one of our dreams.

My eyes sting from the memory and, wow, I haven't cried over my parents in a long time.

Will notices. "Tell me about them."

Even though I'm around a million miles from home, there's something so comforting about this place and the vibe that's going on here in this room. It takes me a minute to identify the emotion: I feel *safe*. I lost my parents when I was sixteen, so it's something I notice. Safety and comfort outside the tiny bubble of my apartment are hard to come by. But that's what it feels like.

Will Finn might be a big, tough, surly wrangler with an edge, but there's more to him than that, under the layers of his smug, gruff exterior. I've met some of his family, who couldn't be more wholesome and generous if they tried, and I can see those traits in him too. His carefulness. His guarded kindness. These details are almost as drugging as the rest of his package: he's *honorable*. It radiates. And what I'm learning is that this is a very alluring thing in a man. Especially when he's as drop-dead gorgeous as this one.

So I keep talking. I take off my glasses and put them on the coffee table. I take out my hair tie, since most of my hair has come loose anyway. "They were beautiful people. The kind of people you want to hang out with, even when you're fifteen and they're parents. They met at a party at NYU, where they both went to college. That's where I went, too, which I'll probably be paying off until the end of time. My mother studied art, my father studied finance. He was a banker. Even after seventeen years of marriage, they were just so incredibly in love, right up until the day they died. I always thought they were lucky like that. It just seemed unusual, to love so hard. They found their perfect match."

"Mine, too," Will says. "They were the kind of people everyone wanted to be around."

"They were?"

"Yeah. They were."

He doesn't offer more information and I don't push him. I let him concentrate. The scratching glide of his brush is soothing. The rush of the river water outside the open window sounds almost musical.

"I hope you don't make me look like a gargoyle," I joke, "to get revenge because I've invaded your peaceful world."

Our eyes meet and he almost smiles. "I'll try not to."

After a little while, I feel my eyelids getting heavier.

I want to keep watching him and appreciating the beauty of this moment, which feels bigger than just us. But before I can stop myself, I fall into a deep, peaceful sleep.

11

WILL

I INVITE her in to see the paintings, even though I know what will happen. She'll make a big deal out of the art, like Fleur did, and drive me insane with it. The problem is, I don't fucking care. It's worth it. I've been craving this for months. I've been *dreaming* about painting a beautiful woman. Not a rodeo groupie, who'll be on her knees practically before she even gets in the door.

I know what that sounds like, and I'm not at all thrilled by my new hang-up, namely having zero interest in a quickie with an easy lay who will beg for more than one night. It's what they do.

I've tried to work from photographs or from memory, but I end up scrapping each one. I've even thought about paying someone, but then news would spread like wildfire around my small town and I don't want the hassle.

They say a head trauma can do that to a person: knock

things in and knock things out. In my case, the severe concussion had several consequences. One, I want a challenge when it comes to women. I want something more than meaningless sex, go figure. I'm not happy about it, but there it is. Two, I started painting. *Again.* Not just painting but *frenzying* in raging creative rushes that last for days. I have trouble sleeping because the urge is so fucking manic. This is totally new. I used to paint sometimes when I was younger, but it was nothing like this.

In fact it has taken over my whole psyche. The only way to relieve the overflowing, pent-up energy is to let it spool out the end of my paintbrushes. I've painted everything I can see. Everything that's a part of my world. But the one thing I really *want* to paint ... I can't. Because of the first problem. I know if I invite one of the local girls back to my studio, she'll never want to leave. And I'm really not in the mood for a melodrama involving tears and tantrums and all the rest of it, which always go with the territory.

I'd almost given up and accepted defeat. Maybe landscapes and rampaging bulls are what I should stick to.

But the cravings kept getting worse. Much worse. Possibly because I haven't seen any action since before the accident.

Not that I *can't* get it up—in fact, I'm having the opposite problem. I've been so mired in lust for the past few months, it has literally changed my personality. My brothers keep telling me to loosen up, to go out to one of the bars in town and pick up a couple of willing one night stands to ease the torment.

But I can't bring myself to do it.

Something has changed.

Me.

And I have no fucking idea why.

Which is why the situation at hand is both a jackpot and a nightmare.

This sassy little city nymphet shows up on my doorstep, out of the blue, like she's made to order. No, *better* than made to order. I couldn't have *dreamed* up a more perfect model if I tried.

The first thing I noticed about her was how outrageously out of her element she was. The second, her face, partly hidden behind her trendy glasses. Her skin is so flawless she doesn't look real. It almost hurts to look at her. She's cute but also sexy in a way she's completely unaware of. Her body is slim but curvy in all the right places. Sort of *ludicrously* ideal.

You can tell she's not particularly experienced. She doesn't have the fuck-me-now vibe of the rodeo groupies. This girl is more buttoned-up. Which is also part of my problem.

I want to *un*button her up. I want to set the little librarian's wildcat free.

I can already tell the sex would be mind-blowing. I'm not sure how I know this, but I do. She'll be responsive as fuck. She'll second guess it at first, maybe even protest. Which is turning me on like nothing else could. Women never *protest*. They beg. They plead. They cry because they can't have more than what I'll give them.

She's different. Sort of feisty and defiant in a way that's getting me harder than I've ever been.

And even though I'll never give her what she came for, the anticipation tastes sweet on my tongue. My chest aches, like her challenge and her presence have amped-up my heartbeat. My vision feels weirdly starry, like she's made the world more colorful than it's been in a long time.

She's got all kinds of contradictions going on. This intrigues me, more than I'd like to admit. She's uptight but sassy. Direct but also genuinely sweet about it. It took courage for her to come down here alone. She isn't abrasive about her requests to see the art, but you can tell it's driving her. She wants my paintings badly, I can see this, and I'm beginning to understand what motivates her. The obsession that began as a connection to her father, now lost to her. I get that.

I'm also starting to understand that *my* new obsession is a way to ease the sense of loss I never dealt with. I never grieved my parents' deaths. It's not really a thing we do around here. We get on with things. We remain staunch and we carry on.

The bump on the head jarred something loose, maybe. A need to let it out. To pour the raw, buried emotions onto canvas in splashes of red and green and black. Maybe that's why it feels so personal.

But now, with her, the need is changing.

I want to paint her. *Voraciously.* Not for buried reasons, but for new ones.

I want to see more of her.

All of her.

When she peeled off her top layer I almost lost it. My lust is quite literally driving me mad. Her breasts are full and bouncy, straining against her tank top. The sight makes my mouth water. The outline of her taut little nipples sends my bursting hard-on into pre-cum overdrive. Which is why I've positioned the easel in front of me, so I don't fucking freak her out. Not until after I paint her, at least.

Then she's free to go. More than free to go, *invited* to hightail it back on up the goddamn trail and back to her city life.

Maybe.

The more I look at her, though, the more I'm starting to realize I have a much bigger problem than just lust.

Painting her is giving me an intense kind of relief. *It feels so fucking good to watch her.* To drink in the sight of how fucking gorgeous she is. Her sweet mouth. The color of her hair, now long and loose, with all these different shades to it, from darker auburn to copper gold to honey blond. Like her eyes, with all their jewel-like golden shards. Without her glasses to shield them, I'm even more mesmerized. She's blowing my mind, in a way that makes me want to sit here and stare.

I have a very big fucking problem.

Because the deeper I get into it, the more I realize this is the best painting I've ever done, by a country mile.

I ask her a few questions to keep her talking. She starts to relax. She tells me a little about her life and her parents. I find myself wanting to eat that pink little mouth. Lick her lips. Sink my tongue into all that luscious perfection until she's moaning. I channel my lust-filled urges into the painting, which is already starting to take shape.

After a while, her eyes start to close.

She sleeps. Her face looks young and angelic. Her body is nubile and sweet and so feminine it reminds me of how long I've been cooped up inside this studio, alone.

I keep going. I finish one painting and search around for another blank canvas, quietly, so I don't wake her. I move my easel closer, studying her face while trying not to be over the top or creepy about it.

This girl just walked out of my wildest fantasies and into my life.

Her beauty is painful, almost. Stoking my lust into orbit and inspiring my art in ways I never even imagined.

They say every artist has one. A perfect subject. Someone that ignites their creativity in ways that no one else could.

I want her.

I'll have her.

But what I'm realizing—to my own horror and bliss, in equal measure—is that this girl isn't just my nemesis, because she wants something I refuse to give.

She's also my muse.

12

ELLA

I OPEN MY EYES.

It takes me a few seconds to remember where I am.

Montana.

I'm in that hot artist rodeo hero sex god Will Finn's studio.

I'm on the couch and a blanket has been tucked around me.

I sit up.

Outside the huge windows, it's a beautiful summer day. The river sparkles. The hills are blindingly green. The craggy mountains gleam stoically in the distance.

Montana grows on a person.

The landscape is so picturesque it could be a wall poster, like the one at the travel agency around the corner from Heights. Oh yeah: the gallery I no longer work at. This relieves me, more than anything. I already feel like I've turned some existential corner. I'm on a different road now. I've found everything I need to make things happen. And I've found something else too.

Him.

The guy that shouldn't exist because it's beyond the realm of even my most imaginative fantasies but does.

He's here.

He's asleep on his bed, still wearing his jeans and nothing else. He's lying on his stomach with one arm curled around his pillow. I can hear the gentle rhythm of his breathing.

Even asleep he has the ability to stun me.

Slow down, Ella.

I can't. Something strange and uncontrollable is happening to me. No, something strange and uncontrollable has *already* happened to me.

I'm hooked, is what I'm realizing.

How could I not be? Just look *at him.*

The broad shoulders, smooth and tanned from the hot summer sun. The wild hair. The sculpted arms. The strong, work-roughened hands, flecked with paint.

Wow.

I get up.

There are three new paintings.

Three? He must have stayed up all night.

I stand there in front of the first painting, staring.

Holy Mother.

It's simply the most brilliant piece of art I've ever seen

outside a museum, still wet. And so's the next one. And the next. They're masterpieces. In each one, I get a different treatment. In the first, my face is painted almost abstractly, except for my eyes, which are startlingly realistic. There are dashes of pink on my face and gold leaf in my hair. The second and the third are done with different colors in slightly different styles. Both make me look angelic and otherworldly.

He's so freaking *good*. It's overwhelming. Not just the beauty of these paintings, but the beauty of ... *me.* Will has painted me almost lovingly, handling everything about me with a sort of over-the-top flattery.

Is that the way he sees me?

God.

If he does—and even if he doesn't—I'm in trouble here.

I *can't* fall for Will Finn. I'm leaving within the next few days, never to return. Most likely without any art, because he was very definite and crystal clear about the fact that he's not interested in exhibiting.

Are you really going to give up that easily? Where's the gumption we know and love about Ella Mackenzie Parker?

It's confused.

It's having issues, because of the second reason I refuse to fall for Will Finn. He'll eat my heart for breakfast. Because he's arrogant, aloof, dismissive and far too good to be true.

At least have a fling with him, girl! At least haul your ass out of the convent you metaphorically reside in and get yourself a piece of that prime Montana beef!

I mentally shut down my inner sex goddess, or whatever voice in my head is currently shouting at me. She's obviously starved for some action. I can admit it has been a while. *A very long while.*

I glance at Will. He stirs a little, rolling onto his back.

Oh, hell. The top button of his jeans is undone.

There's a part of me that wants to leave him in peace, like he asked me to. I have an unfamiliar urge to actually honor his request. I don't want to cause him angst. He seems to have enough of it already.

But the art!

Yes. The art is exceptional. Just like everything else about him.

What a waste! To let all that go without even trying.

I have a lot to think about. Which I'll do, eventually. But first: coffee.

I find the bathroom, tucked away behind a large wooden beam. I turn on the faucet and cup my hands to drink some water. It's icy and bubbly, like spring water. I stare at myself in the mirror for a few seconds. I look sort of wild. Sort of ... good. Amazingly good, in fact. Better than I can ever remember looking. Like the fresh air and the sunshine—*and the company of a certain über-beefcake*— have given me a golden glow. I smooth my hair with my fingers. I don't want to snoop but I'd love to find some toothpaste. Cautiously, I open Will's medicine cabinet. The only thing inside is a toothbrush, a tube of toothpaste, a razor and some shaving cream. I grab the toothpaste and use my finger as a makeshift toothbrush until I can locate my bag.

When I return to the studio, Will is still asleep.

I walk past the paintings and stand in front of them for several more minutes. Why won't he show them? Is there anything I can do to convince him? Or should I book my return ticket today and get the hell out of Dodge? To live with my regrets until my dying day?

No. I'm not ready to go yet. I want to stay a little longer.

For more than one reason.

Shutting all thoughts out of my head, because I don't know what to do about any of it, I go to the door and carefully close it behind me as I make my way down the stairs.

Pulling my phone out of my pocket, I try to check and see if there are any messages, but the battery's dead.

Will's house is nice. Rustic but with all the mod cons. There's lots of wood and a stone fireplace that takes up all of one wall. Huge windows make the most of the expansive views. There are leather chairs and couches and his massive TV. There's a dining room area with a deer antler chandelier hanging over the table, which seats ten. On the table sits a Western-style saddle and one of those things that goes on a horse's head when you ride it that I can't remember the name of. A harness, maybe. Will's hat and chaps are on the chairs where he left them. The room is open plan and I make my way toward the kitchen end, where there's a wooden chopping block island and stainless steel appliances.

The house is as nice as Fleur's, or even nicer. The difference is, Fleur's had a decorator's flair to it that made it homey and inviting. Will's house is very much a bachelor pad and I can't help it, I find myself thinking: *the things I could do with this place. If he didn't mind. We could decide together. I could bring him the color swatches and the fabric samples and*—what the hell?

Slow waaay down, girlfriend.

A large black dog with brown eyebrows notices me and gets off the couch to come over and sniff my leg. I remember her, from the night before. "Hi, Pearl."

She wags her tail, licks my hand once and returns to the couch.

I find a coffee machine and start the brew. Maybe Will wants some too.

There's an iPhone charger on the counter. I plug in my phone. After a few seconds, the low battery image appears. I wonder if we're even in range.

I can hear voices, outside the house. The door opens and someone walks in.

Whoa.

Another brother, I'm guessing. He looks a lot like Will,

but he's blond and lankier than Will. He sees me and does a sort of double-take. He's gorgeous, and in any other time and place I'm sure I'd be starstruck. But I happen to *already* be starstruck, more deeply than I even know what to do with, like it's happening at some deep, cellular level that has changed everything about me, linking me to Will in a way that makes me ... miss him.

His brother's expression is open and sunny, matching his straw-colored hair. It's easy to see that he and Will have very different personalities. He walks over to me, smiling easily. I notice then that he's carrying my bag, which he sets down. He holds out his hand. "I'm Jack," he says. "Jack Finn. Will's brother."

I shake his hand. It's rough, like Will's was when he touched my face. The thought of that moment with Will makes my stomach do a funny little flip. "Ella Parker."

"Nice to meet you, Ella Parker." Jack is still smiling at me, sort of playfully checking me out. "Casey wanted me to deliver your bag to you. She said Fleur's been trying to call you."

"My battery died. I just plugged in."

"You're not from around here." It's more of an observation than a question.

I look down at my outfit. I'm still wearing my punished faux-suede pants and my white tank top, which is lacy and fitted and was never really intended to be an outer layer. But it is what it is and I can't really worry about it right now. "You can tell?" I laugh a little because, well, I'm in *Montana*. And I love Montana. "I'm from New York."

"Wow, New York. Never been. What do you do in New York?"

"I'm an art curator. My boss sent me out here to see Fleur's exhibition."

Jack contemplates me for a few seconds and it makes me wonder. Will's own brother must know about his paintings—or does he? I know Will is secretive about them. "How was it?"

"Spectacular."

A few questions hang unspoken in the air. *What are you doing at Will's house? Are you with him? Did you stay with him in his loft?* I'm glad when all he says is, "You making coffee?"

"Yeah. It just finished brewing."

Jack opens a cupboard and gets out four mugs. He pours coffee into two of them and hands me one. Leaning against the counter, he takes a sip, watching me. He's wearing a faded red t-shirt, jeans with a thick leather belt, and well-worn cowboy boots. His skin is deeply tanned and his irises are the color of dark chocolate, which, when paired with his very-blond hair, is kind of striking. Nathan, Will, Luke, Jack. What I'm thinking is that Montana is like a factory for ultra-masculine hunks. The Finn brothers' parents obviously had some seriously killer DNA going on.

"So," he says, "you work for an art gallery?"

"I used to. Now I'm in the process of starting my own gallery. Well, not quite *in* the process. Yet. But I will be in a matter of weeks. Fleur's thinking of exhibiting with me, which I hope is what she was calling me about." I'm rambling, and it almost sounds foolish. When I describe what already feels real to me, it comes across more like the pipe dream it actually is.

Jack takes another sip of his coffee. "So you're *thinking* of starting your own gallery." Like Nathan, Jack seems to already have a knack for shining a mega-watt spotlight onto my greatest insecurities. "And poaching Fleur," he adds.

Shit. It sounds horrible when he says it like that. Even worse, it's true. I feel the need to clarify a few things to him. "My boss is a total jerk. Any promotion he does for Fleur will be all about his own interests, much more than hers. She deserves better. And I know I can do that for her. I have experience, I know the market, and my contacts are just as good as his, or maybe even better. I know I can get more money for each painting than he can, and I can also get her the kind of publicity that's current and relevant and will lead to bigger opportunities. So I want to try."

Jack smiles. His eyebrows disappear under his blond hair. "Fair enough."

Just then the front door opens again. In walks what could only be yet another brother. He's younger, maybe twenty-one or two, with dark hair like Will's, but it's longer. He's lean and has a loose, reckless vibe. He's, again, insanely good-looking, which I'm practically getting used to around here. He slides his sunglasses up his head and his eyes fix themselves onto me, amused. "And who do we have here?"

"Hi, I'm Ella."

I get another handshake. "Hey, Ella. Wyatt." Wyatt glances at Jack, then back at me. "Here's hoping his mood will now improve."

I guess I know what he means by that. "Actually, I came see about his—"

"What is this?" a voice booms from the top of the stairs. "An ambush?"

"Finally, he gets his lazy ass out of bed," drawls Wyatt, pouring coffee into the two remaining mugs. "The new horse is all saddled up and ready for you."

Will comes down the stairs. He's changed into a clean pair of jeans. His hair is wet from a shower and he's wearing a blue plaid button-down shirt that hasn't yet been buttoned. His gaze is fierce and bright green and riveted on me, and the blaze of my longing surges. *Wow.* I realize I'm happy to see him. Not just *happy*. Thrilled and in awe and energized, all at the same time. *What's happening to me?* "I need a cword with Ella first," Will says. "Alone. You two can wait for us outside."

Wyatt glares at Will in mock offense. "Fine." He flashes

me a grin. "But don't keep Dusty waiting too long. He's impatient."

"Ride him yourself if you're in such a rush," Will tells him.

"You know I would if he wasn't such a maniac."

"Will's got the magic touch," Jack explains, for my benefit. He finishes the last of his coffee and sets his mug on the counter.

"Yeah," adds Wyatt. "He's a horse whispering genius, a heroic champion, a god, a guru, and highly worthy of our undying respect and devotion."

Will reaches for Wyatt, but Wyatt dodges him, laughing, and heads for the door. "We'll see you out there."

Jack follows him. "See you later, Ella."

"Bye, Jack."

My phone is finally charged enough to function. It starts chirping with all the incoming messages. But I don't immediately reach for it.

What could Will want to talk to me about?

13

———

WILL

WHEN I WOKE up and found her gone, I almost panicked.

Which fucking pisses me off.

This whole thing is a disaster waiting to happen.

The problem is, I'm powerless to stop it. In fact, I fucking *crave* it with everything I have.

I don't *want* to crave it. I don't want to crave *her*, more accurately. She's a sassy little city girl from the opposite side of the country. She wants something I'm unwilling to give. She's stubborn, bossy and completely out of place here.

And she's getting me harder than a goddamn pillar of granite.

She's cute as fuck, which is irritating me to no end. Some lethal, one-of-a-kind combination of cuteness and sexiness that's ten times more potent than anything I've ever encountered.

Until now.

Even worse, she's fueling some hidden well of my inspiration to the point where I feel like I'm going mad with it.

I need her.

No.

I. Do. Not. *Need*. Her.

I *want* her. I can at least admit that much to myself. I want to peel off that skimpy lace top. I want to open the floodgates of my pent-up lust all over her. I want to hold her down. Eat all that ripe, succulent, luscious beauty. Tease those nipples, taut against the fabric of her tight shirt, until they're pink and sore. Lick and squeeze and suck on those full, bouncy tits. I want to bite her and eat her alive and ravage her until I've had my fill.

I want to take her to my bed, peel off those ridiculous fake leather pants and rip whatever's underneath them with my teeth. Taking my time. Tasting every inch of her soft, perfect skin until she's dazed and sticky-wet and desperate. I want to slide my hot, agonizingly rock-hard cock into all that sweet perfection and fuck her hard until she's moaning and coming sweetly around me. I want to hear her cry my name as I pump my cum into her tight little squirming body as she pleads and begs for mercy.

Fuck.

I seriously don't know where this is coming from.

And I don't exactly care.

After she's sated and sleepy, her dewy skin covered in my spent need, I want to paint her. For days. I want to paint a hundred pictures of her, until the fever that's burning through my brain and my blood starts to cool.

Only then will I allow her to leave.

But will it be enough?

I don't even fucking recognize the thoughts that are spinning through my head.

When I heard the click of the door as she closed it to go downstairs, I checked—even though she didn't realize it— to make sure she wasn't leaving. When she put on the coffee, I figured I had time for a quick shower.

What I wasn't expecting was my reaction to what I found next.

My goddamn brothers.

My very unrestrained, uninhibited brothers who have no boundaries and no limits. They both have a knack, like we all do—for better or worse—for getting women to agree to absolutely anything.

And they're both staring at her. Practically salivating all over her.

This is surprisingly difficult to tolerate.

I keep my cool. Barely. They pick up on whatever vibe I'm giving off. They stare at me like I'm acting strangely. And they hardly even protest when I tell them to get the fuck out, even if I don't use those exact words.

Now that they're gone I can almost breathe again.

Except that she's staring up at me with those amber-colored eyes. She blinks her long lashes at me and it makes my chest ache with longing. My cock hardens and throbs mercilessly.

Fucking hell, this is bad.

My need feels wild and reckless.

I really don't know if I can control this.

I have an urge to sling her over my shoulder like a goddamn caveman and take her to bed now. I would, but it might scare her. She might run.

There's no way in hell I'll risk that.

"What did you want to talk to me about?" she says.

Somehow I find enough self-control to act almost normal. I know what I look like. It's not hard to get women into bed, even if I have been out of the ring for a while. With her, though, I want to do more than that. I want to go deeper and further. I want her to stay—for a week, *or more* —and give me everything I want. So I tread carefully. "I have a couple of things to do today. I'm going to break in this horse. Then I told Luke I'd fix a hole in the fence. Upriver. Some cattle have been getting through."

"Oh."

"Come with me." I have no intention of leaving Ella alone with my over-eager, perpetually-horny younger brothers. "I'm taking the motorcycle."

She's quiet for a few seconds. "I've never ridden on one of those. What would I have to do?"

She has a way of catching me off guard. I'm not expecting the things she says. This actually makes me smile, even though I'm not really in a smiling mood. "You don't have to do anything except hold on tight. I'll drive. You can sit on the back."

Her make-up, if she was ever wearing any, is long gone. She looks young and fresh and stunning. I notice again that her eyelashes match her eyes and her hair. Darker shades mixed with lighter glints of gold. "Is it dangerous?"

I exhale a small laugh. "No. I've never fallen off. Not even once."

"I guess ... a little danger is good for the soul." She smiles at her own little joke, repeating something I said. Usually something like this would bore me, but with her it has a different effect. It *charms* me. Idiotically.

"I guess it is."

She blinks again and bites her lip. The sight of her small, neat white teeth gently biting into the soft flesh of her pink bottom lip causes my cock to get even more painfully engorged, which is saying something. I almost feel like I'm about to fucking come. I could, so easily.

The colors of her, the plushness, the kaleidoscopic glow. She's quite literally lighting up my world. And I have no idea how to deal with it.

"Okay."

"Okay?"

"I'll come with you."

I smile again, without meaning to. "Great."

"Now that Jack brought my bag, I might take a shower. And just check my messages. Okay?"

"Take all the time you need. There's a shower upstairs and clean towels in the closet. Make yourself at home." These are things I've never offered before. In my past life, before the accident, I made a point of doing my partying at other people's houses, so I could leave whenever I wanted to. This is new territory.

"Thanks."

"I'll be right outside. In the pen. You can't miss it."

"Okay."

"Help yourself to whatever's in the kitchen if you're hungry."

"Thanks, Will."

I watch her for a few more seconds, then I leave her to it, even though it's surprisingly difficult to walk away.

And as I'm heading out to the pen where Jack and Wyatt are waiting for me, taking my time so my fucking hard-on deflates by a degree, it's hard to name the ache that seems to have lodged itself into my chest. Anticipation. Relief, maybe. Possibly even ... happiness. Which is fucked up. How can she make me happy? I don't even *like* her.

Do I?

I don't know. All that matters right now is that *she said yes.*

14

ELLA

WOW.

Okay, that was *intense*. No one could ever accuse Will Finn of being subtle or nondescript. The guy is a walking, talking hunk of big, hot maleness on steroids.

Unfortunately, all that amped-up beefcake shtick is a waving red flag to the rampaging bull of my neglected inner sex goddess.

He wants me to come with him.

Upriver.

You don't invite someone to go upriver with you if you don't want them around, is what I figure.

Do you?

Even if he is gruff and inscrutable, it seems like there's more to it, although I can't be entirely sure it's not just me and my over-excitable imagination. Whenever I'm near him, I get all these crazily sordid thoughts. Like touching my tongue to his perfect bottom lip. Biting it until he reacts. Running my fingers through the dark hair on his huge, warm-looking chest. To the muscles of his washboard abs. To his Western-style belt buckle ...

My thoughts are interrupted by another incoming text. I go over to where my phone is plugged in. As I do, the phone rings.

It's a Montana number. "Hello?"

"Ella? Are you okay?" It's Fleur. "Why haven't you been answering my calls?"

"Sorry, my phone went dead."

"Are you at Will's? Casey said you didn't come back last night."

"No, I stayed here. I slept on Will's couch since it was dark by time we finished talking."

There's a pause. "What did he say?"

"He said no. But I haven't given up quite yet."

"I told you he's as bull-headed as a mule."

"That's an understatement. Luckily, so am I."

Fleur laughs. The question is burning through my brain and I'm grateful when she answers it before I even have to ask. "I talked to Roxanne. You were right. Your offer is a lot better."

"I'm sure she told you about my boss and my former job and the fact that my gallery isn't up and running yet, Fleur. I just want to say that I'll give it everything I've got. I won't let you down, I promise. And I'll release you from the contract if I can't live up to my word, if you do decide to sign with me."

"I've already decided, Ella."

"You have?"

"Yes. I'd like to exhibit with you. I ended up painting all night last night. I'm excited. I believe you."

"Fleur, that's fantastic. Thank you so much."

"Thank *you*, Ella. I know your gallery is going to be a huge success. Why don't you come up to the big house so we can talk about everything? Luke and Casey and Nathan are here. We're going to have brunch. Let's celebrate. If Will's there, tell him to come up too."

"I'd love to. But Will's just gone out to ride a horse, he said. Jack and Wyatt are helping him. Then he said he's going out to fix a fence, and ... he asked me to come with him."

"He did?" Fleur seems surprised by this.

"Yeah. I think he just wants to give me a tour of the ranch or something. It shouldn't take too long. If I can spend a little more time with him, maybe I can convince him."

More laughter. "Good luck with that. When are you going back to New York?"

"I'm not sure. I haven't booked my return ticket yet."

"Oh. Okay. So not today, then."

"No, not today." *I can't leave yet. I'm not ready.* "I'll call you later and we can make a plan and go through all the details."

"Sounds good, Ella. Have fun."

Fleur ends the call.

Holy shit. She's going to sign with me! And I meant what I said. There's no way in hell I'm going to let her down. I know what I need to do. Now I just need to do it.

My phone rings again.

James.

Shit.

I consider not answering. But I might as well bite the bullet and get this over and done with. I take a deep breath and steel myself. "Hi, James."

"Ella. What the hell is going on? I've left you six messages."

"I was just about to listen to them."

"Did you get Fleur to sign?"

"Um ... actually, she's ..." How to word this so it's not a blatant, bald-faced lie? "She's not going to sign with Heights, James. I'm sorry."

"*What?* Why the fuck not? Who's she signing with?"

"Someone new."

"Someone *new*? What the fuck? Goddamn it, Ella!"

For a split second, I feel bad about what I've done. I consider telling James the truth.

But then he reminds me of why I made the decision to break out on my own in the first place. "You've never lived up to my expectations, goddamn it! Not once! I *knew* I should have gone myself! I should have known you wouldn't fucking be up to this!"

Never lived up to his expectations? What could those have been, aside from keeping his business afloat for the past year and a half?

If the unthinkable happens, and I can't get a bank loan or Fleur changes her mind before we can make everything official, I don't want to give James the satisfaction of knowing I tried and I failed. So I don't bother telling him anything.

"You can consider your employment terminated," James huffs. "Effective immediately."

"I sort of figured that."

"And you won't be getting a redundancy pay-out. Since our overheads have been so high lately, I was able to have that clause amended."

Sure you were.

He's still ranting. "The travel agent called and said there's a seat on a flight out of Bozeman that leaves this afternoon at three o'clock. I'm going to confirm that ticket."

"But ... I can't make it by three o'clock."

"Why not?"

I'm going upriver. With a hot genius who I might have already fallen for, head over heels. I want to ride on his motor-cycle. I want to see where the day takes us. Plus I still have things to discuss with Fleur. "I didn't end up staying at the

Super 8 in Bozeman. I'm on a ranch. With dirt roads." Nowhere near my Rent-A-Wreck.

"Ella, it's ten o'clock in the morning in Montana. There's plenty of time to get to the airport to board your flight. Your job there is done. Fucking terribly, I might add. Get your ass on that flight or you can make your own way back to New York. And if the rental car isn't turned in today, the charges are on you."

Fuck off, is on the tip of my tongue, but I hold it. My credit card won't appreciate this but I hear myself saying, "Yeah, I'll make my own way back. Good luck with the Ransom show, James. I hope it's spectacular."

I end the call.

I send a message to Sadie to let her know I'm still alive. I make myself a piece of toast and pour myself a glass of orange juice. Then I carry my bag upstairs to Will's studio and take a shower. After, I comb my hair and leave it down. There's no hair dryer, so I do my best to smooth it into place. It's hot today, with clear blue skies. I brush my teeth. I put on a pale pink sundress with a short skirt, because it's the only outfit I have that might work on the back of a motorcycle. My last-minute packing for the frontier turned out to be an epic fail. What was I thinking with sequins and a pair of high heels? I put on some light mascara and pale pink lip gloss.

I don't bother with my glasses. I don't actually even need them. I started wearing them when I got my job at Heights. People kept telling me how young I looked, which I started to imagine was undermining my credibility or something. I thought the glasses might make me look more sophisticated and worldly, go figure. I'm not sure if they helped or not. But the glass in them is exactly that: clear glass. It's a little ridiculous, now that I think about it. And today, they'll only get bugs splattered against them, probably, at top speed on the motorcycle. At the thought, my stomach curls with nerves. For more than one reason.

I pull on some leather ankle boots with a low heel, which might be a tad more practical for the ranch. Then I go downstairs and make my way out the door.

It's not hard to find them.

I walk over to the large high-fenced pen. Jack is sitting on the fence, watching. Wyatt's in the pen, holding a whip. Will is standing next to a very large black horse, holding its reins. There's a saddle on its back—the Western-style one that was on his dining room table earlier.

"Come on up," Jack says, so I climb up and sit next to him. He takes in my outfit, and my hair still damp from the shower.

"He's going to ride it?" I ask him.

"He's going to try to. The horse is young. He's never been ridden. We always get Will to ride them first."

"Why?"

"They're calmer with him. He's got a way with them."

I can see that about him. That deep, grounded steadiness that was one of the first things I noticed about him. "What if it throws him off?"

"Wouldn't be the first time. But usually they don't."

Will's murmuring to the horse in a low voice, sliding his hand gently along its neck. "Put the whip down," he says to Wyatt, calmly.

Wyatt does, moving slowly to place it on the ground and step back from it, like he's showing the horse he's not going to use it.

Will uses the fence to climb onto the horse. He eases himself into the saddle.

"Jesus. Isn't he terrified?" I hear myself asking.

"A little, probably," Jack says. "It's a wild one. But Will's been doing this since he was about five."

We watch as the horse tosses its head up and down. It looks agitated. It rears up a little.

But Will keeps talking to it in that low voice. He looks completely relaxed, holding the reins loosely in one hand. Then he makes a clicking noise, encouraging the horse to walk. The horse bucks and tosses its head again, but Will holds on, staying secure in the saddle, relaxed and completely unfazed. He tries again, making the clicking sound. This time the horse starts walking around the ring. It snorts but it's obeying Will's commands. After a few minutes of walking around, Will taps his heels against the horse and it breaks into a run. Will controls it, easing it back into a trot. He does this a few more times, somehow commanding the horse to run, to trot, to walk, then trot again. After twenty or so minutes of this rhythm, the horse becomes calmer and more willing.

The whole thing is kind of ... outrageously sexy. The way he can control this huge animal just with the tone of his voice and the squeeze of his thighs.

I'm pretty sure he could control another, much smaller animal with the tone of his voice and the squeeze of his thighs, but I try not to think too much about that. I have a feeling we'll soon find out. I'm almost light-headed with the thought of going on a wild adventure with him. We'll be alone. Just me and Will and all these crazy sparks.

Half of me is terrified, the other half is ... ready. For anything. My anticipation feels white-hot and molten. I try to tone it down because it's not really the time or place to be having this kind of reaction. But I can't. As I watch him, I can't help wondering. Those rough hands. *Will he hold me down?* That surly mouth and the hard stubble of his beard. *God, it might hurt a little. Or a lot.*

Oh, no. It's happening again. My panties are damp, clinging to me intimately under my short skirt.

Now that the horse is obeying him, Will walks it over to

Wyatt. He dismounts and hands the reins to his brother. "All yours," he says. Then he walks over to where Jack and I are sitting.

Will's plaid shirt is tucked into his jeans and thick leather belt. His sleeves have been pushed up past his elbows. The muscles of his arms are defined, even under the layer of his shirt. I notice the flatness of his stomach. He's dusty. His eyes are a surreal shade of green in the full sunlight. He looks glorious. "You ready?" he says to me.

"Yes."

"Where are you going?" Jack asks.

"For a ride. Come on, Ella."

Will has already scaled the fence, jumped down and is now walking toward a barn.

"See you, Jack," I call over my shoulder as I follow Will.

"Don't do anything I wouldn't do," Jack hollers after us.

Will slides open the heavy barn door. Inside is a very large, very scary-looking motorcycle. The wheels have thick, grooved treads. A box-like container is attached to the back, over the rear wheel. "I've packed some food in case we want to stay out there."

"Stay out there?"

"Yeah. You know. Camp."

"Camp?"

He smiles. "Yes. Camp."

"I don't really know how to camp," I explain.

He stares at me. "Don't tell me you've never camped."

"No, never."

"You've never slept outside under the stars on a summer night?"

"No."

"Jesus," he laughs. "Why not?"

"I live in New York City. It's not really advisable."

"Well, you're not in New York City now." He slings one leg over the bike. Then he steps hard on the ... whatever it's called—ignition?—and the motorcycle revs to lusty, smoky life. "Climb on," he says, like it's the least daunting thing in the world.

"Here?" I point to the space behind him.

He's still smiling but his face has this sort of overly-patient look on it. "Yes. There."

I ease myself very carefully onto the motorcycle so I'm sitting behind him.

"Wrap your arms around me and hold on tight."

Wow. I get to touch him. I can smell his scent. Leather and black stallion and sun-warmth, laced with something else. Something drugging and addictive. Him. I wrap my arms around him and clasp my hands tightly. He's unbelievably big and ... *hard.*

"I still need to breathe," he jokes.

I loosen my hold by a minuscule fraction.

"Just kidding. Hold on tighter."

I obey, and just as I do, we start moving forward. *Fast.* The growl of the engine is vibrating through my body, the ground is suddenly zooming underneath us at warp speed, the landscape is a blur, and I'm clutching on to Will for dear life. He steers us out across a grassy field, then up a hill. *Please let me live!* I plead to the universe. What I'm realizing, though, is that he's totally in control of the motorcycle. Like, *impressively* in control. We might as well be on rails, the ride is so smooth.

We climb the hill along a windy path, and Will easily navigates all the grooves that have been baked into the dirt.

We weave through an idyllic glade of trees along a path with a view of the river. The water is turquoise and clean-looking. There's not a cloud in the expansive dome of clear blue sky, framed by mountains. I've never in my life seen anything like the scenery here.

We ride for a while. It's hard to tell how much time passes. Maybe half an hour. A strange feeling comes over me that's hard to name. Contentment, maybe. My arms are clasped around Will. I lean my head against his back.

"You okay?" he yells. The engine is loud and the wind is in our hair. So much for smoothing it.

"Yeah, fine." More than fine. I might be more *in the moment* than I've ever been.

I'm also very aware of the anticipation that's swirling around us, mixing with the engine smoke and the wild, fresh air. A soft, subdued lust is warming me from within. We're all alone, miles from anyone. We're spending the night out here, he said. Under the stars of the Montana sky.

The thought of it doesn't scare me, even though maybe it should. I've only left the island of Manhattan a handful of times in my life. Even Brooklyn feels like the freaking wilderness to me. I might as well be in outer space right now.

With Will, though, I feel safe. I'm already a little in love with him. Or a lot. How could I not be? He's everything I never knew I wanted. A surly, sexy Adonis who also happens to be the next Picasso. What's not to love?

I've decided I'm going with this, wherever it takes me.

I want it to happen. More than that, I want to make it happen.

Will steers us down a hill, alongside the river, where a grassy plain slopes up to a an area of rock formations that look like a high altitude Stonehenge or a portal through time. Even hot, heroic highlanders couldn't make me want to time travel right now. The here and now is too damn good. Too heavy with what's about to happen.

In the middle of the stones, with a nice view of the river, is a small, open cave.

We slow down and Will pulls up next to a fence, where we stop. The high fence is made of rough-hewn logs. One of the top rungs has split and fallen down.

Will kills the engine. "Here's the break."

I unclasp my hands. My arms feel stiff from gripping

him so tightly. I climb off the motorcycle. The breeze is hot and I'm sweating a little, but I miss his warmth. His scent. That feeling of being close to him.

I take in the scenery and the amazing view. If I was ever to try to picture paradise, it might look something like this place. "Can we go explore that cave?"

He grins, and glances up at the cave. "Look who's getting all adventurous."

"I've never been inside a cave before. I've always wanted to see one."

"Never slept under the stars. Never been inside a cave. Sounds like you've been missing out."

Definitely. Something I plan on fixing. "Do you think there might be bears in there?"

He laughs at my earnestness. "It's possible."

It is?

"It's not very deep. They tend to prefer caves that have more shade."

"Oh. So can we?"

"Can we what?"

"Go see the cave."

"How about I fix this fence first? Don't wander off."

He doesn't need to worry. There's no way in hell I'll be wandering anywhere. I don't know the first thing about the wilderness. Or caves. Or bears. "I'll wait for you."

Will takes an axe out of the box on the back of the

motorcycle. "This won't take long, then we'll set up camp. We'll swim. Then we'll eat."

"Okay." Only problem is, I didn't bring a bathing suit.

I sit on a flat rock and watch Will work. He starts chopping down a tree that's the same thickness as the logs of the fence.

The breeze has dropped and the sun is intense. It must be early afternoon by now. Will pulls off his shirt. He tosses it onto the grass and continues chopping the thick tree trunk with his axe. All his muscles are ripped and glistening with sweat from his work.

Hello, Ella from three days ago, who was reading steamy romance novels in the dark of night, fantasizing about this exact scenario. Substitute a hay bale or two with a tree trunk and here we are. Except this is better. Much, much better. Because he's real.

Am I dreaming? I actually pinch myself, just to make sure I'm not.

Once the tree is down and he's sawed off the straggly end branches, Will gets some nails and a hammer. He lifts the log and puts it in place. Then he hammers the nails in to keep it secure.

"There. Now we can go see the cave." He puts his tools back in the box. He grabs a gun and a large bag. Picking up his shirt, he starts walking up the hill.

"A gun? What's that for?"

"Pays to have one on hand, just in case. We see the

occasional grizzly up here. Wolves. Mountain lions. We don't shoot them, just scare them off."

Yikes.

"Come on," he says, like it's no big deal.

I follow him, practically running to keep up with his long strides.

Will sets the bag down near the cave and leads the way inside. "No bears." He smirks at me.

The cave is perfectly oval, like a carved-out little room. It's kind of the most perfect space I've ever seen. "I love this place."

He's so freaking hot when he smiles. "I do too. I spend a lot of time here. Sometimes I'll come out here and camp for a week or two. To clear my head."

"Where do you sleep?"

"Here. In the cave."

"What do you eat?"

"Fish, mainly. The river is full of trout." He nods toward a wooden trunk in the corner of the cave. Next to it are three fishing rods.

"What's in the trunk?"

"Blankets. Supplies. Whiskey."

"Oh."

"I'm going to cool off in the river. You coming?" He starts walking down the hill.

When he gets to the river, Will strips off his jeans,

down to a pair of boxers—*holy hell*—and dives off a rock into a deep pool in the river.

I follow him. Somewhat more timidly, I take off my boots and socks and wade in a little. The water feels icy-fresh. I'm not actually a very good swimmer. I'm fine in the pool or at a mirror-calm beach but this river is *big*. And swift-looking.

"You coming in?" he yells.

I refuse to be an uptight prude while he's frolicking in the river mostly naked having the time of his life.

I peel off my sundress and toss it onto a clean-looking rock. So I'm standing here in my bra and a pair of white lace panties. It's a thing with me: I like lacy underwear. It's one of the few extravagances I allow myself on my tight budget. No one ever sees my underwear, except me, but I like wearing it anyway. I deal with a lot of wealthy, self-important, egotistical assholes on a daily basis so I like to equip myself in whatever ways I can. The glasses are one of my defenses. Knowing I'm dressed like a sex kitten under my work clothes is another. The sexy underwear makes me feel like I've got an ace up my sleeve, like an unknowable X-factor that gives me a tiny boost of confidence when I need it most. So here I am, clad in minuscule white lace and nothing else.

But, hey, it's not like *he* was shy ...

I take another step, but the rocks are unexpectedly slippery. I lose my footing. I fall in. *Shit.* Before I can worry about how awkward I'm going to look clambering back onto the rocky shore, the strong current starts swirling around me, pulling me deeper.

Oh my god.

I try swim back to shallower water but I can't.

The current is too strong and I can't find my footing.

I'm pulled under.

There's no bottom to stand on, and the water starts pulling me downstream. I manage to break the surface and gasp for some air before I'm dragged down again.

Fuck! Is this how it freaking ends? Just when it feels like everything's beginning?

I'm scared.

I'm terrified.

I can't breathe.

I'm scrambling to find something to hold onto but there's nothing but water. Cool, fast-moving water.

Just as I'm starting to really panic, a hand grabs my arm and yanks me up. I'm hoisted out of the river. Will pulls himself—and me along with him—onto a flat rock slab, so he's lying on top of me. We're both breathing heavily.

He's above me. His hair is dripping little diamond droplets onto me. He pushes my wet hair back from my face. "Ella? Fucking hell. Are you all right?"

Am I? "You just saved my life."

"It gets shallower a little further down. You would've been fine."

Would I? I was running out of air.

"Don't tell me you don't know how to swim." He seems upset. "You should have told me that."

"I'm fine at the YMCA."

"The what?"

"I almost just drowned."

"I wouldn't have let that happen. You're okay now. I've got you."

His stunning face is staring down at me. His lips are wet and so luscious-looking I don't want to wait any longer. I almost just *died*, after all.

I weave my fingers into his hair. Will kisses me. Softly at first, then hungrily, like something in him has turned. There's a ferocity to him that's brimming and hot. His tongue licks into my mouth, tasting me in soft, greedy licks. His aggression is measured, like he's trying to be careful. But he can't hold back the wildfire rush any more than I can. He deepens the kiss, his tongue sinking into my mouth, stroking my own. His hand brushes across my breasts, easing the wet fabric of my bra down to frame and plump them from below. He swirls each beaded nipple between his fingers, gently tugging and kneading until it's nearly painful, scalding me with prickling, deepening heat until I moan.

"Ella, I can't take this. You're so damn *beautiful*," he says, his voice low and husky.

He sucks my nipples carelessly, one then the other,

almost manic in his lightness. His mouth moves lower and I squirm as his hands hold me down and peel off the lace of my panties.

Oh. He's so freaking strong. And aggressive.

"Holy fuck," he growls. I started waxing—completely—a few months ago and he seems sort of mesmerized. For exactly one second. Then his mouth is on me and *oh my god,* I've never been kissed *there* before and I gasp as he licks my pussy in greedy, lusty strokes. "You taste so fucking good."

His tongue circles my clit as his fingers swirl the moisture. Then he sucks my sensitive nub into his mouth as his fingers stroke and slide inside me. The rush is sudden and overwhelming, flooding through my body in a crazy-hot torrent of shattering pleasure. I writhe against his mouth and his hold. It's too much. My pussy clenches around his fingers in rippling waves as he sucks on my clit gently, spinning my orgasm deeper. "Good girl," he's murmuring. "Give me everything. Beautiful Ella."

Once the waves start to calm, he climbs up my body and presses his immense, hard-as-stone cock against my slippery, still-pulsing pussy. He's somehow shed his boxers and *he's so freaking big.* It scares me and thrills me at the same time. It's *huge* and thick and wet. Another deluge-of-pleasure orgasm is waiting there. Waiting for him to push himself inside, to find the trigger that will completely undo me.

I'm drowning in my lust for him. And my love. I don't care: I fucking *love* him. I love everything about him. I love what he can do. *I love what he's doing right now.* I want him like I've never wanted anything in my life. The rush of emotion brings tears to my eyes, which mix with the water dripping from his hair. He reaches with his hands to roughly spread my legs wider.

"I want you," he whispers, sliding the broad, slick head of his cock against me. I think I might die from raw need.

Will kisses me again, thrusting his tongue into my mouth, the slippery friction lush and hot. I suck on his tongue and he groans.

He pushes the head of his cock barely inside me. I can feel his *huge* thickness beginning to stretch me. *Holy hell, it's the eighth wonder of the goddamn world!* The sensation is dizzying and my vision blurs at the edges.

"Is this what you want, Ella?" he murmurs in my ear, biting the soft flesh of my lobe between his teeth. "Say it to me."

"Yes," I gasp. "*Please.*"

"You need to be sure because if I go any further I won't be able to stop. I'll give you as much pleasure as you can handle and then some. But I've never done this without a condom and I don't have any. Is this what you want me to do?" He pushes deeper.

"I'm on the pill," I gasp, half-sobbing from the strung-out need of my body as I thank some goddamn lucky star for convincing me to stay on it even when I didn't need to be.

"Good. Because you're going to come around me so hard I'll have no choice but to fill you up with my hot cum. Is that what you want?"

Oh my god. "Yes. Yes."

He slides deeper. But my tight body resists him. I'm wet and needy and half-mad with desire, but *he's too big*. He catches my moans with his kiss. "Relax for me, Ella. That's my girl. Let me in."

He lifts slightly, taking my breast in his hand, plumping it to his mouth. He laps at my nipple with his tongue, circling around the tight nub. Then he bites me, very gently, scraping the edges of his teeth against my skin, kissing, biting and nuzzling his face against me. He does the same to my other breast as he continues pushing himself more aggressively, deeply, thickly, into me, in and out, then in again, finding an insanely beautiful rhythm.

Just when I think I might break from the stretching overload, he settles deep with a forceful thrust.

Will's groan hums, and I know he's fully inside me now. It's almost uncomfortable, this extreme fullness. I wriggle and clasp my hands to his back. Tilting my hips just slightly, I can ease the sensation of being *too* full. I ease barely forward, then back again.

Will pushes his face into my neck. He makes a low

sound, like an agonized growl. "Hold still, Ella. Don't move."

The muscles of his back are strained and rock-hard. I run my fingers across his skin, scratching slightly, teasing him with little pinching caresses. I tilt my hips back again, then up to him. And again.

"*Ella*," he says sternly. "Hold yourself still."

"Why?"

"You obliterate my control," he says, and there's a rough rasp to his voice. He lifts his head up to look into my eyes and we lay like that, still and quiet. "I have never, *ever* felt this good," he says. "And I'm about to fucking lose it."

"So lose it," I whisper.

He's staring into my eyes in a way that's breaking my heart. *I'm making love to him. And I love him.* It's the most intense thing that's ever happened to me. "Not until you do," he whispers back.

He kisses me, and his mouth is hungry and possessive as he thrusts himself into me.

Will hears my soft exhale, reading there the response I'm beginning to find as he keeps his pace steady and controlled, forcing the ecstasy higher. "Let go, Ella. Come for me, baby."

He lifts one of my arms over my head, then the other, locking both my wrists easily in one of his powerful hands. My legs are fully bent, clasped around his waist.

I'm pinned under him, held down by him, impaled by

him. His mouth takes mine. I can only submit to him. He's all I can feel or remember. And as soon as I embrace this total submission, a beautiful current begins to fill my body and my mind. Will's deeply nudging strokes force it higher, melting me completely until there's nothing left of me except this overloading, devastating pleasure. My body clenches tightly around him, squeezing the thick length of him in rhythmic bursts, until he's mindless. I've never felt this happy, as his liquid warmth pools hotly into me, flooding me with sensation, triggering another wave of brimming pleasure.

It's a long time before either of us can move or speak. We're dazed and entwined, completely connected in every way it's possible to be.

15

WILL

HOLY HELL, is all I can say.

She's so sexy it's blowing my mind. She comes at the drop of a goddamn hat. And she's just ruined me for anyone else.

Which would be a catastrophic thing to realize if she wasn't under me, with my cock hotly wedged inside her tight little body, already hard again.

My little librarian *is* a wildcat. Not only that, but she's an angel. Sassy with the sweetest edge. Her breasts are creamy handfuls of perfection. Her body is lusciousness incarnate. I can't get close enough. I have this perverse desire to *stay inside*. I want to pump her full of my cum. *Again.* I want to mark her with my gripping hands and my biting teeth. I want to possess her and eat her alive.

She's watching me with this near-sated, soft expression. Her eyes kill me. The golden shards. The fascination.

Not the kind I used to get, of blind adoration. Ella gives me something more. We have things in common that are bigger than ourselves. We're beguiled by each other and the intensity is mutual, like we're on equal footing.

She *gets* me on a level that no one else ever has, whether I like it or not.

I really don't know what to do about that at the moment. I have a feeling this is going to be a problem, but it's not a fucking problem right now. Because she's coming again. Two of my fingers are gliding over the little puckered cove of her ass, which is slick from my spilled cum. My other hand plays her clit, squeezing gently as I slide my fully-revived cock deeper. She's so fucking *tight*. She's starts gasping and writhing again. Her orgasm works my cock in undulating tugs until it's too much. My own release explodes, flooding her in hot, seedy pulses.

It's extreme, what's happening to us. I've never felt this kind connection to anyone before in my life. Not like this. We need each other, it's as simple as that. It has nothing to do with art or money or a fucking art gallery. This has to do with how hot we are for each other. How hard we make each other come. How much I want her again, now, already. There's a charged, feverish current that makes the thought of any separation from her almost physically painful.

What's happening to me?

We lay there for a while, breathing hard, dazed by this

tsunami of lust and emotion that suddenly feels wildly important. I'm holding her close. We're slippery. We're covered in sweat.

I pull myself from her tight little body. My cum spills. If her pill isn't reliable we'll have some serious consequences on our hands. Weirdly, this doesn't bother me at all. I *want* to be linked to her. I *like* that my seed is deep inside her, that I've come twice, filling her until she overflows with it.

Which is fucked up.

I've never even considered having sex without a condom, in my past life, before everything changed. Now, all I want to do is give her everything I have, all over again.

"Will?" she says softly as I lift her into my arms. I carry her to the small pool near the rocks, where the water is calmer, until we're both submerged up to our shoulders. She holds on tight to me, and I *love* this, which is a new thing for me. I've never felt anything like the things I'm feeling for this outrageously beautiful girl.

"Yeah?"

"I'm glad I found you," she says quietly. "No matter what happens."

My chest feels tight when she says that. Goddamn, *I love her*. She's just so flawless. There's not a single thing I could criticize. Except maybe the sassy little attitude or those librarian glasses, which she's no longer wearing. Actually, I kind of liked the glasses. Even worse, I kind of *love* the sassy little attitude. "I'm glad you found me, too, baby."

Fuck it.

I smooth a strand of her hair out of her eyes. I kiss her soft pink lips.

I just came ridiculously hard. Twice. Deep inside her. I want to do it again.

The magnitude of what's going on here makes me feel wild. Crazy. Like the Earth has just shifted on its axis. My addiction grips me in a tidal wave of need, as though her presence and her beauty is changing the alchemy of my body and soul. She's so damn *gorgeous*, with that multi-colored hair and its tints of dark blond and honey gold, and her spangly amber eyes.

I want to keep her and never let her be alone or afraid or in doubt. I want to make her feel so good she'll never want to leave me.

Shit. I am so fucking done for.

And I don't care.

I rinse her off, then I carry her out of the water and up to the cave. I set her on the warmed stone step and get some towels and blankets out of the chest I keep in the cave, which holds a self-inflating air bed and a couple of duvets.

I wrap a towel around her and wrap another one around my waist. "You hungry?"

"Starving," she says.

I light a fire in the fire pit and set up the grill. I brought some steaks and potatoes wrapped in tin foil, which I stick into some embers of the fire once it gets going. Then I set up the bed, which inflates in thirty seconds. I throw the duvets over it.

"This is pretty deluxe for the Wild West," she laughs. "An air bed?"

"Just because we're camping doesn't mean we can't be comfortable."

"I never knew they could inflate that fast."

"It's the newest model. I bought it online."

She finds this funny and her twinkling laughter makes me unbelievably hard. Again. *Calm the fuck down, man. Jesus.* "You're a very modern cowboy. I like it."

"I've always thought this would be a good place to build a cabin," I tell her.

"I can see why. It's so beautiful." She's watching me cook. I fall harder, for around ten different reasons. The curve of her lightly tanned shoulder. The soft tone of her voice.

I just never imagined it would happen like this. Lust is one thing. Falling *this* hard is a whole different goddamn ball game. I feel like I'm losing my mind. My thoughts feel scattered and ... *sparkly*. Like her eyes.

Fuck, would you listen to yourself?

I keep talking, to distract myself from staring at the lush, full shape of her breasts, which are barely covered by the towel. I want to rip it off and ravage her. Again. "I've already drawn up some plans," I tell her, doing my best to sound less intense than I feel. "It'll be stone and glass to blend into the landscape."

"I'd love to see that."

This is even worse than I thought.

Because the next thing I say is, "I'd love you to see that, too." And I mean it. I want her to help me design it, to stay with me in it, to *live* with me in it.

I don't want to let her go.

Which is a problem.

"We'll stay out here tonight," I hear myself saying, "then, you should stay for a while. With me. If you want to." I sound like a bumbling mess. Because I am. I'm starstruck and besotted, and I really don't know how to handle this.

"I ..." Her hesitation guts me. Is she going to leave? *No. I refuse to let her leave me until I've had my fill of her. Until my new obsession starts to calm the fuck down.*

But what if it doesn't?

"I'd love to, Will. I can stay for a few days."

A few days. I can work with a few days. It'll give me time to convince her to stay longer.

"You should come check out New York sometime." She looks up at me from under those long eyelashes.

Unlikely. But I smile at her, squinting into the sun, which is lower in the sky now. "Not sure I'd fit in."

"It's New York. Everyone fits in."

"Can I bring my dogs?" I joke, and she smiles.

We're quiet for a while, then she says, "Without your art, is what I meant. I wasn't talking about the art."

"I know." She's not hounding me, and I appreciate that. It would be a waste of time, even if she was. "What's your apartment like?" I'm not usually the kind of guy who bothers with small talk, but I'm curious. I want to know more about her.

"It's in SoHo, on Mercer Street. A two bedroom. It's nice. On the small side, but it's home. It was my grandparents' apartment, then my parents', now it's mine."

"So you've lived there your whole life."

"Yeah. I was born there. My mother didn't have time to get to the hospital, as the story goes. My best friend Sadie lives with me now."

As she talks, I'm wondering how all this is going to play out. Her voice has the slightest husk to it, which is sexy as fuck. It's soft and clear and sweet-sounding. It's a sound I don't think I could ever get enough of.

The steaks are ready so I put them onto a plate, along with the potatoes. I only keep one knife and one fork out here, since it's usually just me, so I cut up the steak and offer her a piece, from my fork.

She smiles again, sort of shyly, like it means something that I would be feeding her like this. And it does. I've always been the kind of person who likes total control.

That tendency, with her, has gone into overdrive. I want to be the one she needs, the one she relies on. I want to feed her and protect her.

What the fuck?

I don't care. I do.

She lets me feed her. It's ridiculously erotic, for some reason. I give her sips of whiskey, because it's the only thing I brought, aside from water. I hold my flask to her mouth and she takes a sip. The sight of her wet mouth is becoming too much.

"You're dazzling me, you know," I tell her. "You're kind of blowing my mind."

She blinks at me and smiles.

I ease the tuck of her towel loose, so it falls to her waist.

Holy hell. Her nipples have softened a little and are rosy and ludicrously perfect. I lick my finger. I draw a slow circle around her nipple, avoiding the sensitive peak, until it becomes taut. I do the same thing to the other one. Her eyes get darker and her breathing comes in light puffs. I give her another sip of whiskey and take one myself. She's watching my eyes as I lean closer and kiss her lips lightly. I lick into her mouth. I squeeze and gently play one nipple first and lean in take the other into my mouth, biting softly, licking, sucking on her like I'm drinking her starry essence.

"I have never in my life tasted anything sweeter than you," I say, which just so happens to be true. I'm hooked. I feel hungry and thirsty and feral for more. I want to get closer. I want to take everything.

I ease her onto her hands and knees and she lets me. She's letting me do what I want and this is good because I'm walking some fine line. Some dominating, savage line that would make it difficult *not* to get my way. I like to think I'd stop if she asked me to, but I don't want to be tested. And she doesn't test me. She's *offering* herself, which makes me even crazier.

Positioning her, I ease her head down, so it's resting on the towel. I hold her hips from behind, pushing her knees further apart. Her back is slightly arched and her ass is up, just for me. My towel has come loose and I crouch behind her. My cock is engorged and slick, almost touching her, like it's got a mind of its own.

I plan on *devouring* her, but I'll take my sweet time. I start by slowly licking her sweet pink pussy. She tastes so fucking good I could come right now, but I want this to last. I touch my slippery cock to her pussy, to rub her, dipping into her, teasing her. She moans and arches up for more, but if I keep doing this I'll come right away. And I want her to come first.

So I prod my tongue into the tiny cove of her ass, licking her there as she squirms. I hold her in place and use my fingers to tease her clit. I ease two fingers inside, rubbing her g-spot, playing a rhythm at all three points until her pussy starts clenching tightly around my fingers in soft, undulating pulls.

"Oh, Will," she's moaning.

Everything about her feels so fucking good I know I won't be able to hold on unless I focus purely on her pleasure. I let my cock ease between the slippery lips of her pussy, so just the head's just inside her, being squeezed by the lingering ripples of her climax. I push deeper. As I do this, I use my fingers to play her clit. I work her gently, pulling and kneading the tiny nub. With my other hand, I rub my thumb over the cove of her ass, slick from my tongue, rubbing gently, pressing softly.

Her slick, squirming body is so tight around me it's almost painful. With each lingering ripple of pleasure I slide deeper, letting her inner muscles adjust. *Fuck, she's tight.* I plunge all the way to the hilt in a sleek, driving thrust. She exhales a small gasp, overwhelmed by the gargantuan, throbbing invasion. I slide in and out, pressing deep into all her pleasure zones.

My cock is so tightly rooted inside her it's like a silky, wet, snug nirvana. I want to live like this. Inside my girl. I want to wake up every morning to *this*, to her. I want to eat her pussy for breakfast and feast on her nipples every night. I want to look into those golden eyes and make promises.

I kiss her skin and lay myself over her and grip her

with my hands to keep her there as I thrust deeper than I've been before.

"Oh my god, Will. *Oh, Will.*"

She's coming again and there's no way I can hold on now. Her pussy clamps tightly—*fuck*—milking my cock in luscious, squeezing tugs. My orgasm jolts out of me. Pulsing ropes of my hot cum jet deep inside her. There's so much of it, it spills, wetting her thighs.

I'm keeping her, is all I can think about.

I want her.

She's mine.

16

I'M STILL DAZED. I'm in Will's arms, under the duvet of his air bed in the cave, with its open view to the night sky and the gazillion stars that match the fireworks going off inside my body and mind.

Is there someone I can call and just say, *thank you but I'm signing out now. I'm staying out here with him until the end of time and letting him do whatever he wants to me. Because the things he does are the most life-changing, orgasmic, beautiful things that could ever happen to a person.*

Now I know what I was missing out on. This is better than anything I could have fantasized about or wished for.

I love him, because there's simply nothing about him I could improve on. I love him because I was right: he fucks like a superhero. On steroids. I love him because he's careful with me even when it's his first instinct to be rough. I love him because he's so beautiful it hurts. That he also happens to be the most talented artist I've ever come across is basically icing on the cake at this point.

"Will?"

"Yeah?"

"Thank you for bringing me here."

"Thank you for coming with me."

It must be around midnight. He's still wetly, lazily inside me as he spoons me, his big, perfect body wrapped around me. My endorphin rush has mellowed into an all-body bliss.

"See that row of three stars right there?" He points and I follow his gaze.

"Yeah."

"That's Orion's belt."

"I've heard of it. You can't see many stars in New York City. I don't have much of a view of the sky from my apartment. I've always wished for a roof garden. Maybe one day. Then I'll sit up there and look at the stars whenever I want."

"I took an astronomy class when I was at MSU."

"MSU."

"Montana State. Everyone in my family has gone there."

"What did you study?"

"Agriculture and economics. It was expected that we all

study ranch management. I minored in economics because I was interested in learning how to invest. Turns out, it's not that hard."

"What do you invest in?"

"A lot of things. I wasn't kidding when I said I didn't need the money from rodeo. My portfolio is humming."

I smile because I wouldn't have expected that from him, I'm not sure why.

The light movement of my laughter causes his cock to rear inside me. We've already done this ... *four times*. We're sticky and entwined. We're bonded, that's how it feels.

I've never felt so connected to another human being. Literally or emotionally. It's kind of shocking that I would fall so hard and so fast for this renegade cowboy. But I have. So much that the thought of leaving him—in a matter of days—scares me. A lot. Especially since he's so bull-headed about his refusals to meet me halfway about anything. The art. New York. Any of it.

This really can't end well.

I refuse to think about all that. I don't want to break our spell by worrying about tomorrow.

But I do want to ask him a question, because I might not get another chance. "Will?"

"Yeah?"

"When did you start painting?"

He's quiet for a few seconds, like he's considering not answering me. But then he says softly, in his deep, husked voice, "After my fall. I couldn't work for a few months. I couldn't ride. I was supposed to be on bed rest. Which drove me crazy. I needed something to do."

"Had you ever painted before that?"

Again, he doesn't answer right away. It might be a full minute later when he finally says, "Yeah. When I was younger. But then I stopped."

I'm not sure why it feels like a personal question, but it does. I ask it anyway. "Why?"

"Because there was too much other stuff to do. The ranch work came first."

"But you can't work all day and all night."

"No. It just wasn't considered important."

I'm trying to understand what makes Will Finn tick. And something about this statement and the way he says it, almost defensively, makes me wonder if I've just hit a nerve. "By who?"

More silence. "My father thought painting was a waste of time. For him, everything was always about the land and the stock and all the work that needed to be done. He thought the art was frivolous. And wasteful. Like I was insulting him by painting a picture when I should have been breaking in a horse, or wrangling a steer. He just didn't get it."

And here it is. The answer. The thing that holds him back.

We all have complicated backstories that have a lot to

do with the decisions we make and the people we become. *Here*'s Will's hang-up. He's living under the cloud of what he sees as his father's disappointment, even now.

My father's obsession became my own.

His father's imagined disapproval might be the very thing that's coloring his outlook and making him doubt himself. He thinks the world—or at least *his* world, which is the only world that matters to him—will see his art the same way his father did.

Frivolous. A waste of time.

"I wish I could tell him how good you are. I wish I could talk to him."

Will's gaze returns to the stars. "You and me both."

I don't push him. It seems like he's made up his mind. And it's not really the time—or at least the position—to be psychoanalyzing him about these things. "Will?"

"Yeah?"

"Do you still want to paint me?"

"Like I've never wanted anything in my life." His fingers are weaving into my hair. "Actually, there is one thing I want to do more than paint you."

"What's that?"

"Isn't it obvious yet?" He gives a hint of a thrust with his now fully-revived cock as he kisses my neck.

I arch back against him and the glide of his huge, thick length—*oh god, the thing is a magic wand of orgasm-*

bestowing fabulousness—and it's enough. I can feel the pleasure rushes beginning all over again.

Can a girl ever get enough of this?

No, is the simple answer to that.

There are tears in my eyes as we come together yet again.

Will I ever be able to convince him?

Even more importantly, will I be able to leave him and never look back?

WHEN WE GET BACK to Will's house, he parks right in front of the porch and carries me up the stairs, like I'm breakable, like he can't stand to be separated from me for even one second. I wrap my arms around his neck and weave my fingers into his hair and I kiss him as he carries me.

The two days, by the river, in the cave, have changed us. The more we have of each other the more we want. We've been connected practically the entire time. Coming hard. Gazing into each other's eyes. Touching and tasting and kissing. Learning every curve, every trigger, every pleasure point.

I know what it means when he goes quiet. I know what his breathing sounds like when he's getting close.

I'm so immersed in the kiss I don't notice at first that

Jack and Wyatt are on the couch, watching the huge-screen TV.

Will doesn't even acknowledge them as he carries me up the stairs, kissing me the whole time even as he manages to carry me up the steep wooden staircase.

"Don't mind us," Jack calls out.

They laugh and cheer but Will has already closed the door of his loft behind us. He carries me into the bathroom and turns on the shower. As he's waiting for the water to heat up, he sets me down carefully and pulls off my sundress. My dress is dirty with mud and cum and smoke and whiskey and who knows what else. Like we are. We don't care.

Will kisses me again and holds my face gently. "I'm in love with you." His voice is rasped from emotion and road dust.

"I'm in love with you too." Actually, come to think of it, that ship sailed right about the time our eyes met that very first time right there at the rodeo ring.

He leads me into the shower and soaps me up, washing my hair and my body, his hands gliding over my breasts, down my stomach, between my thighs. He takes his time, touching me everywhere, possessively, like everything about me is *his*. He kneels down in front of me and licks my pussy as I wash his hair. Just as I'm on the cusp of another earth-shattering orgasm, he draws away, smiling up at me slyly. So sexy it hurts. "Maybe I'm going too easy on you. Maybe I should make you wait a little longer. Torment you some. Give you something to daydream about as I paint you."

"No." I sound petulant, for good reason. "I don't want to wait."

He laughs and lays me onto the cedar shower bench. "All right, then. My girl gets whatever she wants."

My girl.

God, I love him so much. Too much. It's too fast and too life-changing. How am I ever going to live without him now?

His mouth latches onto me. He flicks my clit with his tongue. I'm moaning his name and holding handfuls of his hair as the pleasure wracks through my body in electric, excruciatingly-intense waves.

"That's my girl," he murmurs, kissing and licking my pussy so sweetly it brings tears to my eyes.

Once the ripples have calmed, he stands up and puts some conditioner through my hair, working it in.

His cock is hot-looking and dusky. It's so hard it's upright all the way up his stomach. I sit up and I take it in my hands, easing it toward my mouth. "I guess I need to get even. I should torture *you* a little, just for threatening me like that." I lick the crown. I suck on him like he's a lollypop, swirling my tongue.

Will groans. "Don't worry, you're already torturing me."

I take some of the shower gel from the pump on the low shelf and I soap him up. I go slow, and I can see it *is* torturing him. He's very close. So I purposely avoid a rhythm, to make him wait. I rinse him. Then I kiss him again, licking lightly. I take more of him into my mouth, suckling gently. For all the lovemaking we've done, I haven't actually done *this*. I want to. It's crazy how much of him I want. His body, his seed, the beat of his heart. I want it all.

I take as much of him as I can but he's too big and I'm new at this. So I use my fingers to explore him as I suck on him and try to take him deeper. I flick my tongue as my fingers rove. His cock jerks and floods my mouth in thick, hot bursts.

God, there's so much of it. I swallow some. It's the most extreme and intimate thing, *drinking* him, like I'm taking his energy and his life force into myself, letting it feed me and transform me. I'm his. He's mine. We belong to each other. These details feel shockingly real and true.

I swallow as much as I can. Then I lick him, nuzzling and kissing him, *feeling so much for him,* tears mix with the rivulets of water and his milky essence.

We let the water rinse us clean. Will pulls me up and holds me. He stares into my eyes as he recovers and his breathing begins to slow.

He kisses me. "You. Are. Making. Me. Crazy," he says slowly, enunciating each word.

I laugh because I'm happier than I've ever been.

He turns off the water and dries us with clean towels.

Then he carries me to his bed. He arranges me the way he wants me, touching me lightly. Everywhere. "And now I'm going to paint you."

"I'm all yours, genius."

Will narrows his eyes and gives me a look. Then he pulls on a pair of shorts. He finds a blank canvas and sets it on an easel. It's sort of fascinating to watch him as he squeezes different colored paints onto one of his palettes and chooses a paintbrush.

He pulls up a stool and takes a swig of whiskey out of a bottle. He turns on some music. Old school jazz, with the volume low.

And he starts to paint.

I lay here, relaxed, giving him everything he wants. I don't ever remember feeling as *content* as I do right now.

It's late afternoon. Outside, the sun is low and there are some clouds moving in. I'm glad we camped last night, when the skies were clear.

Will paints for a while and I think about how strange it is, that I'm here, with him. That my life has become *this*.

The things that will need to happen over the coming weeks feel too rife with questions that need to be answered. So I block them out, taking the time to just appreciate this moment and how beautiful he looks as he works.

After a while, he says, "I want to explain a few things to you."

I wait, catching his gaze, giving him time.

"Just so you know what you're getting into. In case you want to steer clear."

"It's a little late for that," I point out gently.

"I want to explain why I won't exhibit my paintings. So you know the reason."

"Okay." I'm already ridiculously in love with him. To learn that I've earned at least an inkling of his trust makes my heart feel heavy, as though it's literally overflowing.

"I told you I painted before, when I was younger. I fought against it, and tried to ignore it, but it just wouldn't leave me alone. So I painted when no one was watching and I hid them away. My mother knew and she used to encourage me."

Already I have a million questions. But I don't want to interrupt him. He's opening up to me. *He's letting me in.*

"From the very beginning, it used to piss my father off. If anything interfered with work on the ranch, he wouldn't tolerate that. If he caught me painting, he'd give me the strap, like he used to do sometimes when he was particularly fucking feral about teaching us right from wrong. He saw it as a weakness. He had no time for it and I understood that. I *agreed* with him. I didn't *want* to be doing it. I'd do anything to distract myself. To stop thinking about it. But I couldn't. It was always there."

He pauses for a while, and just when I wonder if

maybe he's changed his mind about telling me all this, he continues.

"When I won some junior calf-riding competition, when I was around twelve, my father was so proud. Finally, it was something I could do better than anyone in my family that I didn't have to hide. So I kept at it. Hoping it would jar the whole art thing out of my head. For a while, it worked. I started getting sponsors, winning every ride, making money out of it. It was something my father could relate to and boast about and add to his list of family accomplishments. It was the only reason I did it, to earn his approval. I never blamed him for not getting my art, not at all. To him, I was selling myself short by indulging some fruity whim that wouldn't earn me respect in this town, which was the only one that mattered. He and his circle of staunch, hard-headed ranchers, who could tell you about the price of beef and the change in the weather but were completely uninterested in anything else."

"I can understand what held you back." The soft music glides on the breeze that's coming in through the open window. It's cooler tonight. I pull the sheet up a little.

"His family, and my mother's family, they were all ranchers. For four generations, on both sides. They worked the land. That's what they did and that's all they did. My family didn't travel. You don't go on vacation when you've got thousands of head of cattle that need constant attention. When you're building your houses and laying your fences and raising five kids. We worked the land. That's what was expected of us. So when my mother once suggested art school, my father went ballistic. It was ranch management or nothing. He and I fought about it."

Another pause, longer this time. I wait for him to continue and when he does, his voice is layered with his grief and his regret.

"It was right around the time I was getting ready to apply for college. I had this crazy idea that maybe I might do something different than everyone else. Maybe I'd pave my own way. Well, when he heard that, he just wouldn't have it. He told me he'd disown me if I pursued some flaky dream that had nothing to do with reality. I told him fine, he could disown me all he wanted. He stormed out and left. He and my mother were going to a cattle auction in town. My mother had been crying because he wouldn't budge and the two of them had words about it. Because of me. And that was the last time I saw them. They never saw it coming and they never came home that night. A fully-loaded cattle truck hit them head on and they were both killed instantly."

He takes another long swig of whiskey.

It won't help but I say it anyway. "I'm sorry, Will."

"So I ended up scrapping all those grand plans and following the path my father would have wanted me to take, because it was the only way I could feel better about what had happened to them. It was the only way to make it up to them. Maybe that doesn't make any sense."

"It makes perfect sense."

His eyes meet mine. "I wanted to tell you all this because I want you to understand what stops me. It killed the urge to ever make a fuss of it, or show it, or talk about it, not that I ever wanted to in the first place."

"I can see why you would feel that way."

"You can?"

"Yes."

He dips his paintbrush and glides it across the canvas. "I stopped painting. I finished my degree in agriculture because my father always said we should keep improving our breeding program and learn about the new technology and so on. I took a few economics classes on the side because I could justify that. I could relate it to the ranch and my family's legacy. And then I came home. I went back on the rodeo circuit. I got on with my life, as I was supposed to be living it."

"But then had your rodeo accident."

"Yes, and it almost killed me. Being cooped up in bed for weeks on end was brutal. It gave me too much time to think. The urge to paint became overwhelming. It was the only way I could stay sane. I couldn't stop myself." When Will continues, his voice is quieter. He catches my gaze and his eyes are blazingly green. "But I can stop it from being seen. And I can stop it from affecting other people. I don't want it to affect you, or anyone else. It stays where it is."

"Okay, Will," I say quietly. I'll give him anything he needs. "I can relate to a lot of that, believe it or not. Art wasn't the first thing I was interested in."

"It wasn't?"

"No. I used to want to be an architect." I laugh a little. "It sounds strange now. It's not like my father would have stopped me from doing that. But the art was so much a part of all the memories. It made me feel closer to them, especially him. I knew it would have made him happy."

"We have more in common than we realized, then."

"I guess we do."

"Would you go back now and change your career?"

I think about this for a second. "No, I love what I do. I made my decision and it fits. But if I could go back to being sixteen again, if I'd never lost them, I think I might have chosen differently back then."

My stomach makes a small growling sound. "Shit," he says, putting down his paintbrush. He switches gears, like he's putting all the heaviness of our conversation aside. "Here I was getting all gloomy and psychoanalytical when my girl is hungry."

He stands up and comes over to me. "Thank you for understanding."

"Thank you for telling me, Will. I really do understand. But—"

He touches his finger to my lips and gives me a mock-stern look. His face is heart-breaking. "Come on. I'll cook something."

So I leave it, and I do my best to accept what he's explained to me, even if I don't want to.

It stays where it is.

WILL PAINTS ME ALL NIGHT, even as I sleep.

When I wake up, he's in his bed with me, wrapped around me. It's the position he likes to sleep in, I've noticed, entwining his arms and legs around me like he wants to make sure he's protecting me.

I *love* this. Like everything else about him. Which is about to complicate my life irrevocably. How much compromise will he be willing to make, is the question. And how much am I?

We have a lot to work through in the next ... day. Maybe two. Real life is screaming at me from afar.

For now, though, I ignore it.

Carefully, I untangle myself from Will's arms. I find a shirt of his and put it on, wrapping it around myself. It hangs to the middle of my thighs.

I go to look at the paintings. There are four of them. *Holy hell.* He's not only the best artist I've ever seen, he's also the fastest. It's mind-blowing how art of this caliber can pour out of him in such a rush like this.

The paintings are, without a doubt, the work of a genius.

Just like that, he's taken his art to the next level. When he paints *me,* for some reason, the layers of paint seem to glow and come to life in a way that's new. The expressiveness. The originality. The emotion. It's all there, in spades.

I allow myself to imagine it for a minute. The reactions of the stiff New York buyers and the ego-inflated critics. How they'd fall all over themselves to buy something like this. How they'd stare when he walked into the room.

But it'll never happen. He's made that clear enough.

I wish I could somehow speak to his father. *If only you could have seen what he's capable of. If only I could show you how the world would respond to paintings like this.*

If only Will didn't feel responsible for the tragedy.

I know as well as anyone how the past can color everything about the present. How some days it feels like you're tied to your memories with unbreakable cables that hold you back. How the guilt of still being here has the power to shape you into the person *they* wanted you to be, sometimes at the cost of who you actually are.

I stare at his paintings for a long time, making wishes. Knowing that only a few of them, if any, will actually come true.

Then I go downstairs to make some coffee. No one else

is here, except for Pearl, and the house is quiet. I look in the fridge and find some bread, eggs, butter and fruit. I make us some breakfast and find a tray to carry everything up to him.

When I get back upstairs, Will is still asleep but he wakes as I set the tray down on the coffee table next to the couch by the big picture window. It's raining today, a light mist, and the landscape takes on its surreal neon tint.

"Hey," he says.

"Hey." I glance over at him and the sight of him makes me feel almost stricken with ... a million emotions. Love, because he's so freaking beautiful and his expression is soft and sleepy and playful. Lust, because he's big and buff and hard AF. Awe, because of what he can do. Sadness, because *how can this possibly work out?* "I made you breakfast."

He gets up and—*okay, good morning, all ten inches of rock-hard mouth-watering perfection.* He wraps the sheet around his waist and walks over to me, his cocky alphaness sort of blowing my mind.

Will kisses me lightly before sitting down on the couch. There are some things we need to talk about that should be said, and now seems like as good a time as any.

He starts wolfing down his food and I sit next to him, holding my coffee mug between both hands.

"Will, I can stay for a few days. Today, tomorrow, maybe the day after that. But then I need to go back to

New York. I wanted to talk to you about ... well, what happens after that."

"Stay longer." His comment is light but I can tell that there's more to it. He hates this topic.

And so do I. But we need to figure it out. "I have to find my gallery space. And a job. I can't really wait much longer. Why don't you come with me? Just for a visit. Then we could ... you know, see what happens."

"What's going to happen, Ella? I'll come back to Montana and you'll stay in New York."

God, why's he being like this? "Or you could stay longer. With me."

"And do what?"

Paint. Be with me. Live with me. It's true, the idea sounds unrealistic. It reminds me that I've only actually known him for four days, which doesn't seem possible. He's completely transformed my life like a black-haired, green-eyed wrecking ball. "Make your own path," I say, almost under my breath.

He doesn't react, but his eyes darken. "There's too much work to do here for me to leave. Who do you think would do it all?"

"Your four brothers? I'm just suggesting a—"

"Could you drop it, please, Ella? I'm not going to fucking New York."

Why's he being such a stubborn ass about this? Then again, I'd been warned. "Will, we need to talk about what we're going to do."

"How about this," he says, taking my coffee cup and setting it on the table. He lifts me and pulls me on to his lap so I'm straddling him, displacing the sheet that's covering him as he pulls up the shirt I'm wearing. His hot, colossal cock glides against me and I go instantly wet, *damn him*. He rips open the shirt I'm wearing, sending buttons scattering across the floor. He yanks the shirt off me and tosses it aside. "How about we fuck all day and I paint you all night and we worry about that later."

God.

He's in a surly and dominating mood. He's not about to agree to anything until he gets what he wants.

I'm tempted to climb off him, and storm away. But his rough hands are on my breasts, his teeth scraping and biting my nipple before he sucks hard, pinching my other nipple with his fingers, sending channels of warmth straight to my core. As he does this, he adjusts me—*he's so damn strong*—so the head of his cock wedges inside me. He uses the honey of my lust to wet the broad head as he stretches me, sliding deeper.

"You're mean," I whisper.

"You're meaner," he whispers back. "For threatening to leave me."

"I'm not *threatening* you, Will. I'm asking you to come with me."

"I want you here," he says, holding my hips, "so I can

be inside you all day and all night and make you come hard like I'm about to do."

But what about the rest of it?

I forget about all that as he thrusts hard and deep until I'm fully impaled by him. It's painful. I'm not as wet as he usually gets me first. But the pain is laced with hard pleasure. Too much of it. I try to ease myself up, but he won't let me. He thrusts again, even deeper, and the pleasure-pain blooms. *It's so insanely good,* the way he makes me feel. I don't care if he's rough and stubborn. I cling to him as the rushes start, as his thick heat pulses and spills deep inside me. He kisses away my tears.

"I'm sorry," he whispers as our bodies remain locked in a slick, rippling bond and my heart breaks just a little bit more.

FOR THE NEXT THREE DAYS, I stay in Will's studio with him. He paints me. We have amazing sex, endlessly. Sometimes we eat. We've entered our own zone, like a bubble of lust and art and extreme connection. Nothing else exists. I give him everything he wants. And he gives me everything I want, except for one thing: assurances.

But time continues to pass. We're still avoiding the topic and I'm starting to feel anxious. I don't want to make him angry again, but I also know I'll be hitting my credit card's limit by the time I pay for the rental car and the ticket home, and that my final paycheck—if I get one—will barely cover my end-of-month expenses. I still haven't talked to Fleur, and Sadie's starting to worry about me. I've kept the two of them at bay with vague, distracted texts. But my time is running out.

The paintings he's created over the past few days are astoundingly good. They're works of art that would earn him a place on the world stage, there's no doubt in my mind about that. But, of course, it won't happen that way. They'll stay here, hidden away, like he will.

A door slams, downstairs. There are banging noises. People are laughing and calling out our names. "Come on down, you two. Time to resurface." It sounds like Jack.

I check my phone. It's 9:28 on Friday morning.

Will yells to them to make us some breakfast and tells them we'll be down in a minute. We take a quick shower together, but already it feels like there's a distance there that's being forced between us. The real world wants us back.

We get dressed and we're about to go downstairs when Will sits on the bed and pulls me close, so I'm standing between his spread knees. His hair is wet. He's wearing faded jeans and a worn blue t-shirt, which hugs his muscles and makes his eyes look like stolen emeralds. His rugged beauty takes my breath away.

"I love you," he says. "I love every minute I've spent with you."

This gives me hope and I kiss his lips.

"You're so *beautiful*," he whispers. "Dazzling the hell out of me, like you always do."

But they're calling to us again.

When we get downstairs, Nathan, Fleur, Jack and Wyatt are all there. Nathan's cooking and the others are sitting at the table, arguing over a card game they're playing.

"Looks who's up," smirks Wyatt. "They've finally disengaged."

Not quite. Will is still holding my hand. "I'll disengage your limbs slowly and painfully from the rest of you if you don't watch your step, little brother." But his threat comes out sounding more good-natured than menacing.

Wyatt's face breaks into a huge grin. He glances at Jack. "His mood *has* improved."

It's a little embarrassing. Everyone is staring at us. We might as well have *We just spent three days having non-stop super-hot sex!* tattooed across our foreheads.

"I love your dress, Ella," Fleur says to me.

"Oh. Thanks. I packed terribly for the Wild West." My dress is a light yellow silk wraparound that's the last clean item of clothing I could find in my bag.

"We brought your car," she says. "It's parked up at Luke and Casey's."

"Thank you."

"What a piece of shit that thing is," comments Nathan from the kitchen.

I smile in agreement, but I'm actually grateful it *is* a piece of shit. At least it won't totally bankrupt me. Then again, I haven't seen the bill yet.

"Luke wants all hands on deck at the cattle yards at noon," Nathan says to Will. "It'll be a big afternoon. Two hundred head of cattle are being loaded for sale. Remember?" Will has now had his time off and they expect him to be there, is what Nathan's tone is suggesting, gently. Nathan's watching Will, maybe studying the change in him.

Wyatt, it turns out, is the kind of guy that doesn't have much of a filter. "So, let me get this straight," he says, to no one in particular. "Ella here is an art curator from New York who's opening an art gallery and who Fleur is going to exhibit with. She also just spent the last three days upstairs with a reclusive maniac whose loft just so happens to be bursting at the seams with crazy-ass art. Any developments we should hear about? Besides the obvious one?"

Okay, wow, nothing like spearing straight to the heart of the matter. And here's the answer to something I've been wondering about all along. They do: they all know about the art, even if he doesn't want them to. Of course they would. It's clearly what Will has spent most of his time doing for the past six months.

His family are all staring at him, then me, then back at him again.

"It's none of your goddamn business, is the answer to that question," Will says, pouring coffee into two mugs and handing me one. Then he goes outside and sits in one of the chairs on the porch in the sun, like he's had enough questions for one day. I already know it's a topic that pisses him off.

Fleur pats the chair next to hers. I sit. Jack is sitting across from me. Wyatt's at the far end, shuffling a deck of cards.

"No luck?" Fleur asks. Jack and Wyatt also seem like they're practically bursting with curiosity.

I guess it depends on what kind of luck she's talking about. "He doesn't want to exhibit. It's okay."

"I'm sorry, Ella. That's disappointing. I told you he's bull-headed."

I *am* disappointed, but I can't bring myself to be too cut up about it at this point. There are too many other amazing things about what's happening between me and Will. The art doesn't seem quite as important as it did. I found him, that's what really matters. Whatever happens next, *he exists.*

Fleur pats my hand and squeezes it. "I talked to Astrid, like you suggested, Ella. Thanks for giving me her number.

She told me about all the artists you've found. And about how good you are at what you do. We can just put something simple in writing for now, and you can send me a contract as soon as you have one. I trust you. I'm excited to work with you."

"She's been painting all night," Nathan says from the kitchen, serving up the food onto six plates.

"That's fantastic, Fleur. I can't wait to get started."

Fleur asks the obvious next question. "When are you going back to New York?"

"Soon. I—" Shit. My voice catches. There's a sting behind my eyes. I almost feel like I'm about to cry, which is terrible, especially with all of them watching me. I take a deep breath and do my best to get it together. "Tomorrow. I have a lot to do before December."

"What does *he* say about that?" Jack says, nodding his head toward the porch.

"I hadn't actually decided until just now. He doesn't—" I'm distracted by another text. From Sadie. She's already sent me three this morning and I haven't had a chance to read them. I need to call her.

"Don't tell me he's just going to let you walk away," Jack says.

Damn it. My eyes start stinging again. "I don't know, Jack. We haven't really figured it out."

"Food's up," Nathan says, and starts setting plates down in front of us.

Will comes in and we eat and the subject changes to cattle and horses and when the hay will be cut.

Which I guess means there will be hay bales. And five hot brothers slinging them around. The hottest of all is sitting next to me, watching me. "All right?" Will says, maybe detecting a change in me. I'll tell him I'm leaving as soon as we're alone again. And I'll tell him I'll come back, when I can afford to, which could be a while. If he wants me to. He told me he loved me, after all.

The thought of leaving him is ... excruciating. I'm so in love with him my head is spinning. My heart feels like it's tripled in size and is pumping a lot of hot, fast, zingy blood through my veins. He's enlightened me. I feel fully *awake* for the first time in my life. My connection to him is the most intense, meaningful thing that's ever happened to me.

I can't just ... not go back, can I? Am I actually considering that? Staying here, living in his studio with him, being his muse and his lover and leaving everything else behind?

It's a ridiculous thing to even consider. My life is in New York. My *bills* are in New York. I can't leave Sadie alone to take care of everything. She can't afford it any more than I can. Together, we barely scrape by.

And meanwhile, Will refuses to budge. Can I figure out a way to *make* him budge? Do I want to?

Yes. I have to. I have to at least lay everything out so we can decide what we're going to do.

Tonight.

Even his family seems frustrated with the line in the sand he seems to have so decisively drawn. There's a tension on Jack's face that clashes with his sunny hair. He seems sort of deep in thought.

Will and his brothers get ready to leave to do their work. Fleur and I go out onto the porch with them.

Will puts on his hat. "You and Fleur can talk. I'll see you in a few hours. Okay?"

"Okay." I want to say more. I want to tell him I love him, but there are too many people, too much noise and too much going on.

He twirls a strand of my hair around a finger. Then he lets it drop and walks away. To his motorbike, which is still parked where we left it.

Jack comes over to me. He's standing very close to me. "Please forgive me in advance for what I'm about to do," he says.

"What do you mean?"

"It might be the one thing that will break him out of his idiotic mindset." Jack places his hands on both sides of my head, under my hair, softly but firmly. I notice again the contrast of his dark eyes and his white-gold, sunlit hair. Very gently, Jack kisses me.

I'm shocked. My impulse is to pull back but he antici-pates that. He holds me in place with his hands and deepens the kiss. His tongue skims my lips.

He's pulled away in a sudden, violent yank.

Will's holding the front of Jack's shirt in his fist. He looks huge and mean, his muscles clenched. "What the *fuck,* Jack?" Will pushes Jack away, hard, so he stumbles down the steps and lands in the dirt.

"If you're going to let her walk away, let me have her," Jack says, climbing to his feet.

"What are you talking about?" Will walks toward Jack, but Jack doesn't seem fazed by this, like he's already resigned himself to getting beaten to a pulp.

"You can't control what happened," Jack says. "It wasn't your fault. You need to stop treating their deaths like you did it. You didn't fucking do it!"

Will stops in his tracks. He looks staggered.

"And you need to stop treating your art like it's some kind of fucking curse. It's not a curse! It's a gift! Don't you think we *all* wish we could do what you can do? I wish *I* could paint like a goddamn genius. I wish *I* had the opportunity Ella's offering you. Mom and Dad couldn't have known where it could take you, Will. *Dad* couldn't have known. But if he was alive today, we could all enlighten him."

I can tell by Will's face that Jack's words are cutting straight to the heart of whatever guilt Will's been mired in for so many years.

"And here," Jack flicks his head in my direction. "Another gift. *Look* at her, man! She's fucking gorgeous.

And you're about to let her walk away, like a goddamn fool! So I want to make sure, before you drive her away with whatever fucked-up shit is going on in your head, that she's sure it's you she wants. If it was me, I know for damn sure I'd be on the next plane to New York."

Jack takes a step toward Will, jabbing his finger into Will's chest. "Don't be a fucking pussy, man! Cash it in! You can't let guilt hold you back anymore. It's too big a price to pay. It wasn't your fault! Do you hear me?"

Will and Jack lunge at each other, throwing punches. *Landing* punches.

Oh my god.

They're rolling around in the dirt in a furious, muscle-bound blur, fighting and swearing. After a few seconds of this, Will gets on top and starts punching Jack.

"*Will*," I plead, running down the steps. "Stop! Please!"

Wyatt and Nathan pull them apart and I notice then that a blue pick-up truck is driving up in front of the house.

It's Luke. "What the hell's going on?"

No one answers. Will's lip is bleeding and Jack is doubled over, breathing hard. They both already have the beginnings of a black eye.

"Where the hell have you been?" Luke demands. "We've already started loading."

This information seems to jolt them out of their stand-off. Nathan pulls Jack up and shoves him into the back seat of the double cab, sliding in next to him. Wyatt gets into Luke's passenger side and Will revs up his motorcycle. Like this kind of thing happens all the time and they're used to picking themselves up, brushing themselves off and getting on with it.

He's bloody and dirty. And so beautiful it takes my breath away. His gaze meets mine and he places his hand over his heart. And then he peels out, leaving a cloud of dust in his wake.

"Holy shit," says Fleur.

Before I can recover, my phone rings. It's Sadie. "I better take this. It's my best friend and she's been trying to get me all morning."

"Go right ahead."

God. My heart's still beating fast after the Fight Club remix. "Sadie."

"Ella. Finally. Did you get my texts?"

"It's been a crazy morning. I was about to call you."

"Have you booked your flight?"

"Not yet. I will. For tomorrow, I think."

"But that's too late! You didn't read *any* of my texts?"

"No, not yet. Why, what's up?"

"You know that gallery space you've been coveting on Broome Street for, like, the last five years? The one with the perfect windows and the cute shingle sign?"

"Yeah." Of course I know it. I daydream about that space on a daily basis.

"There's a For Rent sign in the window."

"What?"

"Yeah. I knew it would go fast so I called the number."

"You did?"

"Yes. The agent said there's already been a lot of inter-est. So I secured it."

"You what?"

"I have it on hold for you. But you need to pay for it by tomorrow."

"What? Sadie, I can't pay for it by *tomorrow*."

"Ella, you own a two-bedroom in SoHo. All you need to do is free up some equity."

"I've freed up a lot of equity already. To keep it."

"Use more. Do whatever it takes. You'll need to get here tonight. I've made two appointments for you in the morning. There's a loan officer at our bank that works on Saturdays. You're meeting with him at ten o'clock. Then you're meeting the property manager at the Broome Street gallery at twelve o'clock. She'll have the keys and the paperwork ready for you to sign. It's yours if you want it badly enough, Ella. All you need to do is to get here. They won't hold it any longer than that. At least *try*, Ella."

I will. Of course I will. "I'll be there."

"This is it. I know it, Ella. This is what you've always wanted."

"You're right. I do. I really do."

"I'll see you tonight, then?"

"Yes. See you tonight. And Sadie?"

"Yeah?"

"Thank you."

"You've spent the past ten years being my therapist and putting a roof over my head, bestie. It's the least I can do."

"I love you, Sade."

"Don't get all sappy on me, girlfriend. Just come home and make this happen. Okay?"

"Okay. Yes. I'll call now and see about a flight."

"Hurry up. Sounds like you have a lot to fill me in on when you get back."

I take a deep breath. "Yeah. I don't even know where to start."

"At the beginning, maybe. See you soon."

We end the call and I'm reeling.

"So you're leaving today?" Fleur says. "I heard most of that."

"I have to leave *now*. Fleur, it's the perfect space. You're going to love it. The light is incredible. Your paintings will look amazing in there."

"Check the flights. I'll write up a quick letter just so you have something with my signature on it. Will that be enough?"

"Of course."

I google the flight schedule. "Shit. There's only one seat left today. It leaves at one fifty p.m."

"It's almost twelve o'clock now, Ella. You better hurry. Go get your bag. You can make that."

"But—" What about Will? I can't just leave without saying goodbye.

Fleur reads my thoughts. "I'll tell him. I'll explain why you had to go in a rush."

But we haven't talked through the things we need to talk about. We haven't made plans about when we'll see each other again.

Maybe it's best this way. For him. He doesn't want to come to New York. He doesn't want to exhibit his art. He's fighting with his own brother over the problems you've introduced into his life, for God's sake. Maybe it's best for him if you make a clean break and leave him alone.

No. It can't be best.

But I have no choice, if I want to at least try to turn my lifelong dream into a reality.

"I don't even have his phone number, Fleur."

"I'll read it out to you so you can key it into your phone."

I enter Will's phone number into my contacts list.

"Hurry, Ella. It takes forty-five minutes for *me* to drive to the airport. Your car will take longer. Plus you have to return it. And check in. Go pack."

Will I make it in time? I go inside and up the stairs, throwing all my things into my carry-on. I find a scrap of paper on one of his tables, and a pencil.

. . .

Will,

A space has opened up for my gallery and if I don't sign for it by noon tomorrow, I'll lose it. I have to try. I'll call you when I land.

I love you.

I'm sorry.

Ella

I LEAVE the note on his bed and take one last look around his studio. The place I spent the most beautiful week of my life.

Then I grab my bag and I close the door behind me.

17

ELLA

NEW YORK IS HOT, dirtier than I ever remember it being, and so crowded I can barely make my way through the throngs without bumping into people.

My time in the wide open country of Montana has changed me. The tall buildings, for the first time ever, feel oppressive. The city heat that radiates off the sidewalks, even at this time of night, is stifling. By the time I make it to my building, I feel like I'm covered in a thin coat of grime.

I get home and Sadie's there, with her long dark hair and midnight-black eyes. She's beautiful and exotic-looking and wise beyond her years. She's been my family, my guide and my best friend, all rolled into one, for the past ten years.

She hugs me and we talk for a while but there's too

much to explain, and it all feels raw and more intense than I can handle after the long day of travel.

"You're tired," she says. "Tell me the rest tomorrow. Get some sleep."

I hug her again. Then I go into my room, which is so familiar, yet suddenly seems completely different. *It* hasn't changed, I realize. It's me who's changed.

I hold my phone in my hand and I sit down on my bed. My heart's beating faster.

I love you. I can still feel the blaze of his eyes as he whispered the words to me.

I call him but it goes straight to voicemail.

"Hey," I say, feeling awkward, now that I'm a million miles away. "It's me. I hope you're okay. Call me back."

I take a long shower and collapse into bed. I check my phone.

No messages.

THE BANK APPROVES my loan and I decide to add more to it to pay off my credit cards and give myself a buffer. And a plane ticket. Turns out I have more equity than I thought. It's surprisingly straight-forward and I arrive at the gallery twenty minutes early.

I stand outside on the sidewalk.

I check my phone for the thousandth time. Still nothing. Even though I've left two more messages.

The gallery is as cute as it's always been, if a little neglected on the inside. The windows are dirty. There are hooks and wires on the bare gray walls. But the space itself is raised and wider than it is long, so the windows run the length of the entire space. The glass is slightly irregular. It's that bullet-proof kind that can't be broken into. Which is good. If I have anything to do with it, priceless artworks will be hanging inside within a matter of weeks.

I jump when a woman comes up behind me.

"Are you Ella Parker?"

"Yes, hi."

"I'm Valerie Atkins. With Gotham Properties."

She unlocks the four deadbolts on the door and lets us in. The place is dusty and the lights don't work but I don't care.

I'm visualizing the clean white paint, the spotlights, the strings of fairy lights in the nook where the drinks table will go. The bold, vibrant paintings.

I sign the papers and Valerie hands over the keys.

"Congratulations," she says, and shakes my hand. "Good luck with the business."

"Thank you."

She lets herself out and I stand there for a while, walking slowly around my new gallery.

Look, Dad. We did it.

I sit in the middle of the floor and I let the tears fall. I never used to be much of a crier, but this week my emotions have been on overdrive, along with everything else about my life.

It feels good this time, to let it out. And to breathe it in.

Whatever happens, I know I'll be okay.

I'll work hard. I'll create a thriving, global sensation of an art gallery.

But first, I'll go back to Montana and tell him I don't want to live without him. If he decides then that it was just a flash in the pan, a week of insane chemistry and stellar orgasms—and that's *all* it was—I'll accept that, like I accepted his damages.

But I'm going to do everything I can to convince him otherwise.

I think I've got a pretty good shot.

I try his number again.

I'm surprised when he picks up on the first ring.

"Ella? Jesus, where *is* this place?" *Will. God, his voice.* He sounds gruff and out of breath.

"What place? Where are you?"

"Broome Street. That's what Sadie said. But she wasn't sure of the number. I googled you and tracked down your address."

Broome Street?

It's then that I see him. Standing in front of the window talking into his phone. He turns. He sees me. And he smiles. All beefed-up, sun-tanned six feet and three inches of him.

I let him in and he scoops me into a bear hug and starts kissing me like he does ... *when he's already inside me.*

My black-haired, green-eyed hurricane genius beef-cake lover is back.

Then he breaks the kiss and glares at me sternly, blinding me with his cowboy glory. "What the hell are you trying to *do* to me? You *leave* me? After I told you I *love* you, you turn around and leave me behind? What the hell's *that* all about, Ella?"

I laugh because he's so damn beautiful and my love for him feels like it's bubbling up and spilling over. He has a black eye. And his tantrum is the most adorable thing in the world.

"I was about to come back," I tell him. "Tomorrow."

"I couldn't wait that long."

I notice then that he's holding a bottle of champagne in his hand. At his feet is a carry-on backpack and also a huge black bag, the kind you might carry skis in.

"I passed a wine store on the corner." He pops the cork. "We have some celebrating to do."

"What's in the bag?"

He grins at me. "Guess."

"What? Will ..."

"Jack was right. *You* were right. I brought twenty-five of them. And there's plenty more where that came from."

I'm stunned. *He brought his paintings?* "Are you sure? You don't have to."

"I know. But I want to. It's time to pave my own road. Doesn't mean I can't do all the things I've done all along. It took finding you—and losing you—to realize that I've been wrong about a few things. And there was no way in hell I wasn't coming after you."

I touch his face, avoiding the angry bruise around his left eye. "That looks sore."

"You should see Jack's."

I wince at the thought. "How is he?"

"He'll live. He's talking about coming over for the exhibition opening. I told him fine but if he ever pulls a stunt like the one yesterday, I won't go so easy on him next time."

Very, very gently, I kiss his bruise. "I love you."

"Good. Because you're stuck with me. We're going to make this work and get everything we want."

He kisses me for a long time.

"Thank you," he says. "For opening my eyes. There's so much I want to say to you, but we have time."

Yes, we do. *We have time.*

"Come over here." I pull him by the hand.

We sit and lean against the wall.

He raises the bottle. "To our mothers." He takes a sip and gives me one. "And to our fathers."

We drink to our lost parents. And we, finally, lay our grief to rest. I guess it took finding each other to somehow figure out that we had bigger destinies than the ones we were allowing ourselves. Now, the future feels wide open.

Will takes another long sip. "And here's to all the babies we're going to have."

He pulls me onto his lap and we drink to our future.

"When can we get started?" he says, wrapping me in his arms, touching his warm, champagne-flavored lips to mine.

Five months later ...

THE TWENTY-FOUR PAINTINGS Will painted of me during that week in his studio ended up being his first exhibition. Everyone agrees they're some of the most important, innovative paintings of the decade. He kept his favorite one— the first one—but all the others sold for crazy prices. And I mean *crazy*. The total amount from the sales is a number that's hard to even think about. Even my small cut is more than I ever thought I'd see in this lifetime. His next exhibitions, scheduled for March and April, are on track to make him the first billionaire artist of the century. I'll take some credit: my marketing tactics have been exceptionally successful. Not that it's hard to market a rugged rodeo hunk from Montana. The New York buyers have been all over his paintings like pigs in mud.

And the crowds have been all over *him* like bees to honey. But he's mine and I'm careful with him. He doesn't like crowds. He holds my hand like he needs it for support, which pretty much melts my heart and makes me fall even deeper in love with him, if that's possible. Every day, I discover something new about Will that charms me and slays me. I'm not going to say that he doesn't have flaws. He's human, after all. It's just that I simply can't see them. To me, he is quite literally perfect.

I give him every part of myself. We both know how fleeting life can be, how it can all be over in a second, when you least expect it, so we make the most of each day.

We cook for each other and go out of our way to take care of each other. We talk about our hopes and our fears. Our damages and our dreams. My relationship with Will is the most special and important gift of my life. I don't hold back from him. I love him with my body and soul and my whole heart. And he does the same. He tells me he loves me around a hundred times a day.

Will bought us the four-bedroom penthouse loft apartment that takes up the entire top floor of my building, part of which happens to be directly upstairs from my own apartment. We're having an elevator installed between the two. The loft is amazing. It has balconies off each of the bedrooms, a larger one off the living area and the kind of light New Yorkers kill for. It even has a roof terrace we're transforming into another outdoor living area. We have a garden, and it's the kind of space I never dreamed could be mine. It even has a hot tub. We got one of those air beds that inflates in thirty seconds and we sleep under the stars when the weather is clear. Sometimes we can even see Orion's belt.

Will and I got married in Montana, two months to the day after we met. There was no point waiting. We knew what we wanted. There are times in life when you just have to go for it, and marrying Will Finn was definitely one of those times.

Sadie was my maid of honor and Astrid and Fleur were my bridesmaids. Will's brothers were his groomsmen, with Jack as his best man. It was by far the best day of my life.

Jack and Sadie seem to have hit it off. Jack is talking about coming to New York to stay for a while. He told me he's never seen Will so relaxed and happy. I'm just glad Will has retired from rodeo. I don't think I could watch him do that again. Not now. Not ever.

Jack and I have become close. There aren't any weird vibes after the kiss and we've all moved past all that, recognizing it for what it was: a tactic to jolt Will past his self-imposed boundaries. I've become used to Jack's upbeat, steadying presence and I love him like a brother.

My new gallery is around the corner from our apartment. Astrid jumped ship at Heights as soon as I offered her a job. She's fabulous. I'm paying her triple what James paid her. She's so relieved to be rid of him, she's like a new person. She admitted she felt horribly trapped in her relationship with James almost from the day it started, but she didn't want to lose her job. She's more confident now, and has found some promising new talent. James got over it by hiring another blond assistant curator, but last I heard, he was having trouble getting artists to sign with him.

Fleur's exhibition is coming up next week and she and Nathan are coming to stay with us. I'm excited. It's nice to have a *family* again. Brother-in-laws and sisters. It's something I'm still adjusting to, but I feel grateful every single day. They're a big, loud, loving family and they treat me like one of their own.

I leave Astrid in charge of the business when we go to Montana, which is often. Will likes to get his dose of sanity every few weeks, as he puts it. We've added some new decorating to his (*our*, he keeps reminding me) house. We're building another cabin on the ranch, too, which is my new favorite place on earth. At our spot by the river. We named the house Upriver. Will and I designed it together. It's modern, and is being built around the rocks, so that some of the walls are the rocks themselves. The rest of the house is going to be made of stone, wood and glass. Our bedroom is the cave. It'll be sealed and climate controlled, with a sliding glass door that we can keep wide open whenever we're there. It's been designed to blend into the landscape and has the most stunning views I've ever seen.

Will bought me a horse and is teaching me how to ride. Her name is Moonshine. She's a Palomino. She's quiet and calm and neighs when she sees me. She eats sugar cubes straight out of my hand. I *love* her. And Pearl is my new shadow.

Will said it's good we have so many houses and bedrooms because he wants to fill them all up with our babies. I said we're going to need to have a *lot* of babies if we want to do that, which just made him smile. We talked about it and I decided to go off the pill around six weeks ago.

Today, there's something I need to tell him.

As soon as I get home, I go up to Will's studio, which is in one of the huge bedrooms of the loft. He's listening to music and painting. As always, he looks gorgeous, with his dark hair flecked with paint. He's wearing low-slung worn jeans and a black t-shirt, which hugs every one of his sculpted muscles. I still can't get used to how hot my husband is.

He just started a new series. A New York series. He's taken to the city in a way I wasn't expecting. On Saturdays, we've started our own new tradition, like the one I shared with my father. We walk around the city and look at the galleries and museum exhibitions. It's different with Will.

He's so fascinated by each new discovery, taking it all on board, studying the technique and the style of each piece with an artist's eye. If anything, his own style is evolving into something even more original.

He looks up when I walk in. He sets his paintbrush down and stands up. "Come here, beautiful," he says. I walk over to him and stand on my toes so I can kiss him. He lifts me up and carries me to the bed, which he keeps in here so I can help inspire him, as he puts it. Which he likes me to do at every available opportunity.

He holds his weight above me, kissing my lips. "Have I told you how much I love you yet today?" he says, dipping his tongue into my mouth. I suck on it lightly and he groans.

"I went to the doctor this afternoon," I tell him.

He stops kissing me, staring down at me sharply. "Why? Is something wrong?"

"Nothing's wrong. We're going to have a baby."

I'll never forget the look on his face as long as I live. Of pure happiness and undiluted tenderness. There are tears in his eyes. I've never seen Will cry before. "I can't believe it. I love you so much. I can't believe we're going to have a *baby*, Ella. *Our* baby."

He lifts my shirt and starts kissing my breasts. He unhooks my bra and sucks adoringly on my nipples. He kisses a trail down my stomach.

"Hey, little baby," he murmurs against my stomach. "I'm going to take such good care of you and your mommy and give you the best life any little girl has ever had."

I laugh. "How do you know it's a girl?"

"I just think it is. What should we name her?"

"We have time to decide. The baby isn't due until September."

"Let's name her Rose."

"Rose?"

"My mother's name. What was your mother's name, Ella? I've never asked you that."

"Mackenzie. It's my middle name."

"We'll name our baby Rose Mackenzie Parker Finn."

"That's quite a name."

"It's perfect."

It *is* perfect. And so is he and everything about my life, now that he's in it. "What if it's a boy?"

"We'll worry about that for the next one."

I laugh again at his certainty. He's peeling off my jeans and my panties. He pushes my thighs apart and nuzzles me, licking me intimately.

"I love you," he whispers, playing me and sucking me until the pleasure becomes too much and I shatter. He keeps licking me until the ripples ease. Then he unzips his jeans and kicks them off. He lays himself over me and slides his huge cock deep inside me. As always, the thick, sleek glide rubs against every sweet spot I possess. I wrap my arms and legs around him, holding him as close as I can as we come together. For a long time, we kiss and stare deep into each other's eyes.

"I love you so much it hurts my heart," I tell him.

"I love you so much it breaks my heart," he says, then he kisses me again.

EPILOGUE 2

ELLA

Five years later ...

"Mommy, the baby's kicking again." Rose loves laying her head on my swollen belly, feeling the baby kick. She's four now and is my little helper. She sings to the baby and talks to it, telling long, rambling stories. She's the most beautiful child I've ever seen, even if I am biased. She has hair that's not quite strawberry blond and not quite platinum, but somewhere in between. Her eyes are the color of golden amber. "Daisy likes it when I talk to her."

"Daisy?" I laugh. "How do you know it's a girl?" I remember having this conversation with her father not too long ago.

"I just know. Daddy thinks I'm right."

"I'm sure he does." Rose adores her daddy, but she likes to stay with me when he's out on the ranch. She's not interested in ranch work and prefers drawing. In fact, it's very obvious she's inherited some—or a lot—of Will's talent. I don't want to jump the gun but some of the paintings she's done might already get noticed.

Seventeen months after Rose was born, I gave birth to identical twin boys. We named them Cooper and Samuel. They have black hair and bright green eyes. They're stunning little hell-raisers and aren't happy unless they're following their daddy around like adoring puppies. Will takes them everywhere with him.

I hear their footsteps on the porch steps and their laughter as Will helps them take off their muddy boots. They scamper in and climb onto me, covering me with kisses.

"Careful now," Will scolds them. "Daisy's due any day so we need to be gentle with mommy."

"I want to see Daisy now," says Coop.

"Me too," says Sam.

Will carefully lifts them, carrying one under each arm. "You'll get to meet her soon enough. Come and sit at the table, you three, and I'll make us some dinner."

I smile up at my gorgeous husband. "You and Rose seem very sure about this." We decided not to find out the gender of the baby. I like the surprise.

He leans down to kiss me, lingering. "I'm always right," he murmurs.

"Our daddy loves our mommy so much," says Coop.

"Yeah," Sam pipes in.

"That's because she's so beautiful," Rose tells them wisely.

"The most beautiful mommy in the whole world," Will adds.

I didn't know it was possible to be this happy.

Our little Daisy is born one week later. She looks just like her sister.

We stay in Montana, where there's more room for the children to run and play. When I can, I go back to New York to check in on Astrid, who now runs the gallery for me full-time. I can manage things remotely, but she's more than capable, and I have enough to keep me busy. We ended up buying the gallery, and the building it's in, when it came up for sale. We've expanded it into the second and third floors. The gallery has become one of the most sought-after in the city.

Will still paints in the evenings, after the children have gone to bed. His paintings now hang in museums, royal palaces and in the houses of movie stars, glitterati and art collectors around the world.

Sadie and Jack are living in our New York apartment, and there's plenty of room for family, who visit them often. Nathan and Fleur spend time there with their little girl, Haven. Fleur exhibits with us at least once a year and has also found global success, although not anywhere near Will's. Luke and Casey have four children now. Their second-oldest, Ava, is Rose's best friend. Wyatt seems to be chasing after the ranch vet, whose name is Jasmine, even though she keeps turning him down. Will and his brothers are taking bets on how long it'll take him to convince her.

At night, when the stars are out and the house is as quiet as the house gets, with the rush of the river water outside and the sounds of the animals, Will holds me in his strong arms and whispers love words in my ear, kissing me and giving me the gift of his body, his love, his total devotion. And I give it right back.

Sometimes dreams do come true.

Thank you for reading! If you enjoyed Will and Ella's story, please consider leaving a quick review or rating for **Cowboy**.

Below I've included the first chapter of **Nashville Days**, a sexy standalone small town rockstar romance and the first book in the Music City Lovers series. It's my tribute to hot summer days and finding the kind of love that feels like the real thing from the very first day.

I'm also including the first chapter of **Hopeless Romantic**, a steamy he-falls-first sports romance that's a tribute to love at first sight and insta-everything (because it happened to me :)

xoxo,

Julie

Please come join my Facebook reader group, Julie Capulet's Romantics, where I share cover reveals, insider info and we discuss all things romance!

Sign up for my newsletter to receive my free bonus content and get access to sneak peeks and exclusive giveaways!

Visit my website @ www.juliecapulet.com

Every song he wrote was about a girl he hadn't met yet. Then she walked into his life.

Travis Tucker is a country-rock superstar. With four number one albums, sold-out tours and millions of fans, he's living the dream. But somewhere along the way, the spotlight lost its shine. Travis can never find the one thing he's been writing all his songs about: *real* love. So he decides to buy himself a country getaway to work on his next record and clear his head.

Ruby Hayes is a small town girl with big dreams. Finally free of boarding school, she plans on spending the summer writing songs on the piano in the abandoned farmhouse next door. Then she's on her way to Nashville.

When Travis finds Ruby, singing like an angel at his piano, he falls *hard*. Now that he's finally found the girl he's been searching for, Ruby ignites in him a wild obsession that's hotter than the Tennessee sun. And she has no idea who he is.

For Ruby, things get complicated. With a voice that's somehow familiar, like he's already a part of her, Travis is a temptation she can't resist.

The summer becomes a feverish haze of hot nights, shared lyrics, and the kind of spark that blazes into wildfire.

But summer can't last forever. Can their love survive beyond it, with the demands of Travis's high-profile life, Ruby's ambition and a jealous best friend threatening to come between them?

Or is this a love story written in both the music and the stars?

Nashville Days is a steamy standalone small town rockstar romance starring a hot, hopelessly romantic lead singer and the sweet, sassy songbird who steals his heart. Perfect for fans of Elsie Silver.

Music City Lovers

Chapter One

TRAVIS

"I want to thank ya'll for coming out tonight, Austin. You know we love you." The crowd roars.

We play our last song, our newest number one hit. I can barely hear my own voice as a hundred thousand people sing along with me. It's a crazy feeling, having *this* many souls touched by your words and so fully invested, singing their goddamn hearts out. They know every note. They've lived their lives to these lyrics. They've loved, cried and laughed to these tunes. They're filling up the night with their emotion, swaying to the slow rhythm. The lights of their phones shine like a galaxy of stars.

And when we hit that final chord, the thundering cheer of the crowd is deafening. Vaughn climbs down from his drums and the three of us stand there together on stage for a few seconds, taking it all in. The applause of a hundred thousand people is something you don't ever really get used to. The adrenaline rush is just as pure as it was the very first time.

We take a final bow and exit the stage, where a swarm of security surrounds us and ushers us through a bullet-proof corridor toward our tour bus. I can still hear them chanting my name. But we've done our encores after playing for three and a half hours. We're getting close to the end of our 48-show, 38-city tour and I'm feeling it. The highs and lows and the creeping exhaustion that sets in after giving it everything you've got for months on end. We have two final shows left, both at home in Nashville. It's been by far our biggest tour yet.

I feel lit by the crowd, the music, the whiskey and the wine, the satisfaction of pouring my heart and soul into something real. Something that touches people and connects them. Every single show has been sold out. Our record is number one. Four of our songs are in the top ten. And the momentum just keeps on building.

We get to the bus and it's crowded, with groupies and people from the band and hangers-on. Our opening act, Jackson Cole, and his entourage are here, like they always seem to be. The fame and the women are new to him. He's overdosing and finding his feet, maybe. Riding our wave, to a certain extent, but whatever.

Vaughn pours three shots. Roxie gives Kade a hug, then me. She's relieved. Turns out our little sister is a genius at managing us. This tour has been bigger than we ever imagined. Now we can play our last two home shows and finally take a much-needed break before we start another 12-show West Coast tour next month.

I collapse onto one of the plush chairs. I tip back the whiskey Vaughn hands me. One of the groupies puts her hand on my arm and leans close to me. "Travis, you were amazing tonight. You're *so* good."

Do I know her? I don't think so. She might be a new one. It all starts to blur at the edges after a while. They all start looking the same. I'm no saint but I also need to *feel* something before I'll act on the constant stream of attention and adoration I happen to get. Right now I'm not feeling much of anything.

Kade hands me a beer.

"Hell," he says, sitting in the chair next to mine and clinking his bottle against mine. "Texas always has insane crowds. I could hardly even hear us." As usual, Kade's newish girlfriend Carmen is hovering around him. Roxie's not a fan. Come to think of it, neither am I. I don't usually care much who my brothers hang out with, but this girl seems to have an effect on Kade that's messing with his head. He's more moody when she's around. Jackson joked that she's our Yoko, waiting in the wings, whispering in his ear all the time about running away together so he can work on his solo album. I don't think that's his plan. Not now, anyway. We're on too much of a roll. And I can't worry about it tonight.

Vaughn laughs and cranks up the music, chugging from the bottle of Jack he's holding. He's got a fat joint in his other hand. A groupie with a lot of piercings and a ridiculously short skirt puts a pink pill on his tongue. Another girl is unbuttoning his shirt. His black hair is unkempt and long. His eyes are bloodshot, which makes them look even more blue than usual.

Roxie pulls one of the girls away from him. "What did you give him?" She pries Vaughn's mouth open but he grins at her, sort of guiltily.

"Too late," he says.

"*Vaughn*," Roxie scolds him. "Booze and weed is one thing. You said no drugs."

"Come on, Rox, I'm celebrating. Give me one night."

"*One* night? You've had three whole *months* of nights."

"I'll go cold turkey after the tour," Vaughn tells her. "I'll take a break."

We've all heard that one before. My brother is out of control, is what it boils down to. And he's only getting worse.

Vaughn has always walked a fine line. Like our father did, until it killed him. Kade and I can easily keep up with our younger brother when it comes to the whiskey—and usually do—most of the time. The difference is, we have downtimes. We lay off when we're not touring. We clean up when we feel like it.

Cleaning up isn't something Vaughn's done in a while. I'm not sure he's even capable of it at this point. Kade and Roxie and I have talked about it. We decided to finish the tour, then we'll sit him down and talk it through with him. Get him some help or check him in somewhere if need be.

None of which is happening tonight.

We're driving all night tonight so we can get back to Nashville in the morning. There's no doubt this party will still be going when we get there.

This bus has been the hub of our non-stop bender all the way through. We all got into a groove of it for the first month or two, but after a while you find yourself getting more and more strung out from the total lack of sleep and peace and quiet. Even before we left, we were hounded like this. We have a loft warehouse we've converted into apartments, a recording studio and an office headquarters in downtown Nashville. We tried to keep the location under wraps but our fans found out about it, like they always do.

"That show was mayhem," says Vaughn. Not that he minds. Mayhem might as well be Vaughn's middle name. As if to confirm this, he blows a couple of smoke rings at me.

Tonight I'm not in the mood to fight my way through crowds of people just so I can go to bed.

What I need is some real sleep. Uninterrupted by banging and knocking and people trying to get in.

I need a quiet place to hang out for a while, I decide. A secret getaway. An old house out in the country somewhere, far from the city and the rabid fans and the never-ending parade of groupies, where there's space and fresh air and days with nothing to do except write. I can't remember the last time I was *alone* for more than a few hours at a time.

I'll find myself someplace off the beaten track, where no one even knows I'm there. I'll sleep and daydream and clear my head. Maybe Vaughn can spend some time there too, and dry out. And Kade, without the girlfriend. All three of us. We'll work on our next record. We'll write our masterpiece, uninterrupted.

I send a message to a real estate agent I sometimes use when I buy new properties. I have three houses: an apartment in Nashville that's part of our headquarters, my own house in Franklin outside Nashville that I need to get a lot more security for because people have set up fucking camps around the peripheral fences, and a condo in L.A. None of them will be either empty or quiet. I have a lot of friends and an open-door policy for the most part, which I'm now starting to severely regret. All my houses have become magnets for hangers-on and their non-stop parties.

I'm looking for another house, I text him. *A farm, maybe, at least a half hour outside Nashville. Something remote. Very private. Surrounded by a lot of land. Maybe with a barn or something I can soundproof and convert into a studio. ASAP.*

Three girls surround me. One of them touches the top button of my shirt. I'm not in the mood to party tonight, go figure. I'm strung out. *Burned* out. I'm twenty-five years old and I already feel like I'm hanging on to the end of a fraying rope. I've been burning the candle at both ends for as long as I can remember and I suddenly feel a new urge for some goddamn solitude.

One of the girls touches my hair. Another whispers in my ear. "You're *so* hot, Travis. I love you so much."

I don't even know her name.

One of the girls weaves her fingers through mine. "We want to show you something in one of the bedrooms, Travis. *All* of us."

My phone pings with a message. It's from my real estate agent. Damn, he's fast. "Maybe later." I don't know, maybe I've become jaded. I don't want to fuck just for the hell of it, not that I ever really did. I'm not an out of control player like Vaughn and I'm not a soulful romantic like Kade. I fall somewhere in the middle. I have a good time without getting serious.

But sometimes—like right now—it occurs to me that I never quite *feel* as much as I wish I did. Never in a way that makes you want to hang on to it or get excited about it or make it last. Never in a way you'd write a goddamn song about. Which is too bad. Because I write a lot of songs. Songs about falling in love and chasing after that one and only true love because you think your heart will break if you can't spend every hour of every day with her until you die.

The truth is, I'm just guessing. Because I've never experienced anything close to that kind of intensity. Which, tonight, feels sort of ... sad. All these desperate souls, looking for that one magical, elusive person they can fall in love with to the point that nothing and no one else matters.

Most of them will never find it. *I* might never find it.

Which is sort of tragic when you think about it.

Like now. Women are literally hanging off me. And I feel exactly ... nothing. No spark. No interest. Just ... boredom. A craving for something *real*.

I stand up and move away, as much as I can in the smoky, noisy, jam-packed space. People are getting loose.

I check the message. *I've got a new listing you might want to see. It's been sitting empty for 4 years and needs some work but it's a premium property. Beaut house. 5 bedrooms. 40 mins east of Nville, remote. Sits on 100 fenced acres with its own pond, a large barn and 3 cabins. Listed at 3.5m. It's bank-owned and available immediately.*

I follow the link and scroll through the photos.

Wow. The place is mint, but he wasn't wrong. It looks dusty and unkempt. In a good way. In a no-one-will-ever-suspect-I'm-there kind of way. I'll leave it like that. I'll become a hermit for the next few weeks and completely tune out. There are pictures of the barn too. It's huge and rustic. And the old cabins, dotted around the property.

The offer is almost too fucking good to be true.

I text him back. *Let me know where to transfer the $. I'll pay cash tonight.*

I'll move in immediately. Hell, I'll drive out there as soon as we get back.

We exchange a few more messages. He confirms that the sale has gone through. He'll have the power turned on. He'll courier the keys so they're there by the time I get to Nashville.

A strange longing settles into me that feels almost like hope. More than that. An eerie sense that something's about to happen...

When he falls, he falls *hard*.

Millie Baylin just moved to a new city to start college. Introverted and studious, she plans on spending most of her time holed up in the library working on her novel and keeping to herself. But when she gets dragged along to a school football game by her fun, football-mad new roommate, the hot quarterback almost drops the ball at his very first sight of her.

Bo McCabe is saving himself. A hopeless romantic at heart, he's holding out for the real thing. As soon as he lays eyes on the shy stranger with the striking gray eyes and the angel's face, he'll stop at nothing to find out if she's the one he's been waiting for all along. Millie thinks Bo's insta-obsession is insanity and wants nothing to do with him. But Bo is determined. Because, somehow, Millie has already stolen his heart ... and he is now utterly obsessed with winning hers.

Can Bo convince Millie he's the man of her dreams?

Hopeless Romantic is a sexy standalone sports romance starring an obsessed quarterback and the love of his life (includes two HEA epilogues!).

Chapter One

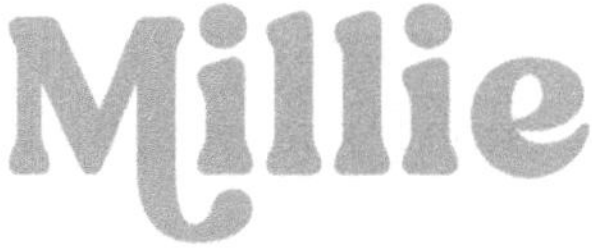

The bus drops me off next to the front entrance of the university.

I walk up to the main admissions building, where I'm given a map and a bag full of booklets and welcome materials. I make my way through the crowd of people on the campus green, keeping my hat low over my eyes, using the map to try to find my way to my new dorm.

I can't believe I'm here.

College.

I never knew if I'd actually get this far. So many times along the way, college had seemed like a place *other* people went, a goal not just up among the stars, but over in someone else's galaxy. But I've made it. This is *real*. My dream, against all odds, has come true.

I graduated from high school more than a year ago, but it's taken me this long to save up enough money to get started. Desperate to get as far away from my hometown in Florida as possible, I applied to four schools. *And I got in.*

This place is like a different world. More than forty thousand students go to this university. It's practically its own city, with top-ranked sports teams, space-age libraries and students from every walk of life you could imagine. It's got an energetic, optimistic vibe to it that's kind of blowing my mind. The autumn air is crisp and cool. People are pink-cheeked, wearing colorful scarves, holding steaming cups of coffee and hot chocolate from a nearby coffee truck. Until two days ago, I'd never in my life been north of Atlanta. Everything about this place feels new and exciting and picture-perfect. I almost feel like I belong here.

Belonging isn't something I've had a lot of experience with. I don't fit in or make friends easily. Not because I intentionally try to be an outcast, but because I'm used to keeping secrets.

But not anymore.

All my secrets have turned to dust.

Here, I'm not the poor kid with a heroin addict for a mother. Or the lonely waif who lives in a trailer park and carries Narcan in her pockets. I'm not the freaky teenage girl who wears hats and oversized jackets in August to hide myself because I live alone, or close enough. My only protector was too far gone to care.

All that's behind me now.

My mother is dead. It feels like a mercy. The needles, the wasting away, the giving up of every shred of herself just to get her next fix. I tried to save her, but she just couldn't be saved. Grief was weaved into the painful fabric of our downward spiral. Which meant that, as soon as she was gone, it was surprisingly easy to walk away. I'd already said my goodbyes to the person my mother was, a long time ago.

Now, I'm *free.* Free of the pain and sadness of my past.

Today, here—right this minute—I can start my new life.

In this mini-city of forty thousand people, I know I can find my own quiet corner, where I'll be perfectly content to watch everyone else having the time of their lives while I get to work and do what I came here to do. Kick ass, in the only way I know how.

It's a strange thing to have a knack for. As soon as I started writing stories, something clicked. When I write, I enter this fever dream that takes me into other worlds. I use writing to crawl inside my own mind. To escape from reality. It helped, when I needed it most.

The coffee-scented air leads me over to the coffee truck. I stand in line. I'm wearing my usual loose jacket and my black sailor's cap that I tuck my hair into. Because I actually *need* them in this weather, which is a nice change. People still stare at me. I'm used to it. I know what I look like.

Students are clustered into groups, talking to each other, *meeting* each other. I sometimes wonder, like now, what it would be like to be fun and outgoing. The girl behind me in line starts up bubbly conversations with a couple of random strangers, without even a hint of self-consciousness or turning red or stammering over her words, like I would. Shyness is a curse.

My backstory doesn't help, but at some point, you just have to move on. That's why I'm here, after all.

"What can I get you?" says the guy in the truck. He's staring. I pull my hat a little lower.

"One hot chocolate, please."

He smiles, making no move to get my order. "You must be a freshman. I'm sure I would have noticed you."

"Yes. I just arrived." After three days on a Greyhound bus, but I don't bother with the details.

He pours cocoa into a cardboard cup. "I'm Mason."

"Hi, Mason."

I don't offer my name in return. There's a line behind me and I really just want to get my drink so I can go and find my dorm. But Mason takes his time. "And you are?"

I relent. "Millie."

"Millie," he repeats. "I like that name."

"It's sort of old-fashioned, but it works."

His gaze roves across my face, taking its time. "Hey, there's a party at my place tonight. You should come." He scrawls a number on a napkin and hands it to me, along with my cup of hot chocolate. "Give me a call."

"I'll see. Thanks." I hand him my money card.

"It's on the house," he says. "Really. You should come. It'll be fun. I can pick you up if you need a ride."

"Hey, man," says a guy behind me in line. "How about stop trying to pick up the freshman and make us some coffee instead?"

I take that as my cue. "Thanks, Mason."

"See you tonight, hopefully," Mason calls after me, but I let myself drift into the crowd. I already know I'm not going to Mason's party. I'm not really the party-going type. Besides, I don't have time. Part of being able to afford college came from the advance money for a book I wrote last year, when I was going through the worst of ... the worst. By some miracle, I landed a literary agent, who got me a two-book deal with a major publisher. They said my writing was "heartfelt," which is true enough. The money isn't a huge amount, but it meant I could afford to start college this year, instead of waiting another year or two to save. I have no idea how I'll finish the second book by their deadline of January 1st, but I guess I'll figure it out. That, along with the full course load I'll be taking, means I'll basically be living in the library for the entire first semester.

I check my map, pretending I feel confident and ready to take my new world by storm. At least if I *look* like I know what I'm doing, people might actually think I do.

There's a band playing a Fleetwood Mac song in the middle of the green. Nearby, some guys are throwing a football around.

The sky is blue, with only a few high, wispy clouds. It's late afternoon. The leafy trees are vibrant shades of red and orange, with an artful smattering sprinkled across the green grass. Autumn, like I've only seen it in movies. Everything's so colorful and ... *collegiate*. Preppies, jocks, hipsters and academics are mingling seamlessly, all wearing splashes of the same school colors.

Nearby, a cluster of girls are eyeing up the football jocks. These are the kinds of girls who used to make my life hell in high school. The social media-obsessed types who spend hours making sure their selfies are envy-worthy. They hate people like me: people with problems they don't want touching them and their shiny lives. Loners, who—God knows why, since I avidly try to avoid it —take attention away from them. And it's always the kind of attention I wish I wasn't getting.

I do my best to avoid them. Maybe things will be different in college.

I'm mortified when one of the jocks calls out to me and

starts walking over to me. He's huge and built like a Marvel character.

I try to steer clear but he blocks my way, so I'm forced to stop.

"Hey," he says. He's literally towering over me. I have no doubt he could break me in half if he wanted to. It's intimidating. "Are you a freshman?"

I just had this conversation and I really don't feel like having it again. I'm not good at small talk. "Yes. And I'm on my way to my dorm, if you'll excuse me."

"You're fucking *gorgeous*," he says.

I don't know how to reply to that so I step around him and keep walking but he walks along with me.

He's persistent. "Where're you from?"

I don't want to chit-chat with this oversized stranger. "A small town I'm sure you've never heard of."

"Try me." He's sort of sweaty and bulging and it's freaking me out.

So I hurry past him. "I'm sorry but I'm meeting someone and I'm late. It was nice talking to you."

"You and me should get together sometime," he says.

That's not going to happen in this lifetime or the next twelve, I don't bother saying. I keep walking, hoping I'm heading in the right direction.

"I'll look out for you," the jock calls after me.

Luckily, unless he likes hanging out in hidden corners of the library, he'll never find me.

My dorm isn't far. It's full of people carrying boxes and saying goodbye to their parents. A pang of something that's not quite sadness and not quite jealousy flutters, but I let it go. It doesn't matter anymore that I'm alone. These people are starting their new lives too, just like I am. Some are already partying. I slide past them and make my way up to the third floor.

My roommate is there, sitting on the bed next to the window that has a view out over the green. She's going through an open suitcase and she looks up when I walk in. She has long hair the color of polished copper and a sprinkling of freckles across her nose. Her face lights up, like she's genuinely happy to see me. "Hey, roomie. I'm Violet."

I smile back at her. It's impossible not to. She's fun and nice, you just get that impression. "Millie."

"Hi, Millie. I hope you don't mind me claiming the bed next to the window. And the bigger closet. Your desk is bigger, though. And you have an extra bookshelf."

"No, that's fine."

"I saw you talking to that football player and his groupies," she says.

"You saw that?"

"I was feeling your pain." She laughs. "Those girls' faces when they saw it was *you* and not them he was chasing after."

"Well, they can have him. I hope I haven't already made a few enemies."

"Those girls will be fine as long as you stay away from the football team."

"You know them?"

"I know their type." She sets a picture of her family on her bedside table. She has a lot of brothers, it looks like. "My brother was the quarterback at my high school in Wilmington. My other brother was a wide receiver. And my *other* brother was a halfback. We had girls like that camping out on our doorstep every night of the week."

"Wow. Well, I'll definitely be staying away from the football team," I assure her. "As far away as possible."

"There's no way we're not going to the game tonight, though. You *have* to come with me. I don't know anyone else here yet."

I laugh a little as I put my bag on my bed and start unpacking it. "I'm probably going to skip the game, sorry."

"No *way*, roomie, you can't bail on me! I refuse to sit there by myself and I can't miss the opening game of the season. My brothers would kill me."

"I'm not really into football," I admit. I've honestly never watched much of it and couldn't tell you the rules if my life depended on it.

"What are you into?" Violet's face is open and sunny, like she's actually interested and not just asking to make small talk. So I find myself telling her.

"I'm a writer."

"That's so cool! Are you an English major?"

"Yeah. How about you?"

"Psychology. I'm planning on becoming a shrink. Believe it or not, it's been my lifelong ambition."

"Wow." I start putting some of my stuff into drawers.

"Yeah, just be careful. I might go all Freudian and start psycho-analyzing you any minute."

I smile without meaning to and it feels good. It's been a long time since I made a new friend. "I'll watch out for that."

"If you ever feel like you might need some therapy, just let me know. You can be my first patient."

I take my hat off and toss it onto my bed. My hair tumbles out and hangs past my shoulders. It's been a while since I cut it.

"Wow," she says. "Is that your real hair?"

I have strange hair. It's a very pale shade of red that's almost blond, but not quite. It looks pink under certain lights. A lot of people comment on it or stare at it or want to touch it, which is why I usually keep it hidden. I cut it shorter after my mother died, in one of those weird moments where you do something and you don't know why. But it's grown back since then. I have bangs and it's angled around my face, unevenly in places, because going to a hairdresser wasn't something I could ever afford. "I'm thinking about dyeing it black."

"Don't you dare. It's amazing."

"So's yours." It really is. It's a coppery red with gold highlights.

Her phone pings and she's busy for a few seconds. "So, what do you say? Kick-off is at four thirty."

"I don't know the first thing about football."

"I'll teach you," she says. "Who knows, you might actually enjoy it."

ALSO BY JULIE CAPULET

I Love You Series

The Obsession Begins (free)

XOXO I Love You

XOXX I Love You More

Love You The Most (free)

Sexy Standalones

Max

Cowboy

McCabe Brothers Series

Hopeless Romantic

My Hero

Arrogant Player

Music City Lovers Series

Nashville Days

Nashville Nights

Nashville Dreams

Nashville Lights

Hawthorne U Series

Lovestruck

Paradise Series

Devil's Angel

Wild Hearts

New York Billionaires Series

Billionaire Boss

Billionaire Grump

Billionaire Devil

Billionaire Romantic

Standalone Rom-com

Beautiful Savages

Julie Capulet is an Amazon top 20 bestselling author of contemporary romance. She writes steamy he-falls-first romance with heart, heat and fairy tale HEAs. Her stories are inspired by true love and she's married to her own real life hero. When she's not writing, she's reading, traveling, walking on the beach and watching rom-coms.

www.juliecapulet.com

9 781968 790134